A Bum

To: Rich Curley on his [?]
May your future Bumps be
few and smooth.
Enjoy
Bill Fuller

A Bump on the Road

Contents

Preface 2
The Hump 5
Our Place 11
The Front Row 17
Family Secret 24
Run 29
Guinness of my Childhood 39
Glorious Morn 44
Incident 51
Free Range 59
If Only 65
In for the Day 71
My Dear Boy 76
Big Pol 82
The Deliverance of Destiny 88
A Weak Tummy 95
So You're Off Then? 103
New Neighbour 113
Down Memory Lane 120

A Bump on the Road

Preface

I make the truth as I invent it truer than it would be – Hemingway

To paraphrase Clive James, most first novels are disguised autobiographies. These short stories are disguised memoirs – creative memoirs. Some are closer to being autobiographical than others, but they are all stories – figments of my imagination, including my reminiscing ramble *Down Memory Lane* that formed the basis for the stories. Hemingway suggests that by making them 'truer' is what makes all good books alike.

Michael McLaverty advises to go for the intimate and the local - this I have attempted. Seamas Heaney describes McLaverty's "love of the universal, the worn grain of unspectacular experience, the well-turned grain of language itself" – this, too, was part of the endeavour.

Little nuggets of memories give birth to these flights of fancies. Writing these stories is the next best thing to time travel: exploring that period of childhood through creatively making the memories 'truer' was great fun. Frank O'Connor talks about rewriting stories that have been published, reworking them maybe fifty times. I discovered I was rewriting stories over and over in my head and I am sure I had versions stored on lost floppy disks, almost two decades ago.

Most of these stories emanate from the innocent years before secondary school, and the growing out of it - that awakening provides the richest well to draw from. *A Bump on the Road* reflects an observant child attempting to understand the world around him. Family - parents, siblings, aunts, uncles, cousins, friends, and the wider community: The Church, The Troubles, secrets, ghost stories, leaving home, myths and legends, all this comes under the microscope of a child growing up. A couple of stories deal with going to England and migrating to Australia - moving away from the security blanket that is home.

A Bump on the Road

The boy (and the young man) describes that world with wit and bittersweet nostalgia. The reader is taken on a gamut of emotions in this rich and amusing journey from whooping Christmas joy, childish preoccupation with play, and avoiding boredom, to grief and fear of adults in school and church. This world of small town Ireland is brought evocatively to life by his wonderment of snow, holidays, playing, family, school, church and gradually moving away. Sorrow is never too far away.

The well of childhood is explored through various themes from seemingly routine family activities – *Free Range and Family Secrets*, The Troubles – *Incident and Our Place*, the lore of ghosts – *Front Row and The Hump*, Christmas expectation with a twist – *Glorious Morn* and scrappy street gangs - *Run* to the phenomenon of the show band era – *If Only*.

In for the Day reveals the fear of starting secondary school and the excitement of visiting the big city. It is a tribute to Eamon Friel's folksy, unmistakable voice and lyrics that mirror the Northern Irish earthy mood; a mixture of the melancholy and the craic. *Big Pol* reveals bored pupils against a background of The Troubles.

Other stories included here have some connection with childhood: *My Dear Boy* reflects stark grief when the unthinkable happens. Milan Kundera states we are always children because we constantly have a new set of rules before us such as starting afresh either in Manchester or Melbourne: *A Weak Tummy* and *New Neighbour*.

So You're Off Then, set in Northern Ireland in the early 1900s evolved through looking for William O'Connell and his wife Maggie, my great-great-aunt who migrated to Australia about that time, meshed together with some oral family history told to me by my Granny's sister, Priscilla, when she was 99 years old.

In *The Deliverance of Destiny*, a contemporary piece on migration where the sins of previous generations permeate through to the children.

A Bump on the Road

My thanks to Rosemary for her constant encouragement – it is almost as old as the memories, to Jill for reading, proofreading and making some excellent suggestions, and to Matthew who wants to be the first to buy the book.

Contact me with your thoughts on the stories -
abumpontheroad@yahoo.com.au

© Hugh Vaughan 2009

A Bump on the Road

The Hump

Easing the frozen net curtains off the glass, I drew a circle on the thin ice with my finger and moved the melting water to the bottom of the window. Outside, the frost hung in the air, a gleaming white-out. Everything in the crescent wore a glittering coat, from the road, right up to the shiny sloping roofs and beyond - all a silvery sheen. The wished-for Christmas had come again on seeing this magical sight, instead of the usual dull drip of rain trickling down the windowpane. My frost-free view was big enough to see the crescent, the bulbous cul-de-sac. Two houses, on our side and the same opposite, bordered it. A hawthorn hedge on the left, shrouded in mist, gave refuge to the Big House that once dominated the surrounding fields and cottages.

The owner, a squat man, stood at a gap in the hedge, fixing the barb wire fence. He had erected it to keep out the hoards of boys, intent on filling their jumpers with russet apples from his autumnal orchard. Hoary white on vacant trees and crisp under foot, he checked on his defenses. Thick tartan socks rose out of his laced up boots, trousers tucked snuggly inside, the tight fitting jacket of purple hue buttoned up with black discs, red burnished cheeks on his pale face. Holding a spotted handkerchief, he wiped a dripping nose with an ungloved hand and then scanned the crescent before moving off, unseen, into his garden.

As I watched through my little porthole, someone opposite pulled their red curtains, giving no sight of a body, just movement through their opaque window. Otherwise, all windows in the crescent were covered within and nothing moved without. Steps led to their green doors, with little snow-covered gardens and obligatory centerpiece shrub, a mantle of white. Knee-height concrete walls bordered the footpath, overgrown with privet hedges. Our corner garden led alongside a public path, otherwise most gardens were similar; the hedge ran from our front gate down along the path to a side gate, the entrance into the back yard.

I crossed the chill lino-covered landing to my bedroom. It had two beds - a double and my single, which was covered in several heavy blankets,

A Bump on the Road

its multi-coloured sheets trailing onto the floor, and crowned with a deep-navy quilted eiderdown. Sliding my feet under the covers to find some warmth I knelt to look into the back yard through the damp window, the hanging frost still gathered at the eaves. Below, the shed occupied half of the yard and on its flat bleached roof lay a broken bicycle and pieces of discarded frost-encrusted timber. A wooden green gate led into a narrow vegetable garden, empty of produce, clay turned in the drills, allowing the frost to do its work.

Down the centre ran a cinder path, a snow thickened washing line hung above, attached from the shed to a tree at the bottom of the garden and on it, a solitary tea towel, suspended, fixed in space, benumbed. The line was supported by a proud pole shaped from a branch, fashioned and pared by all, and with its natural hook, a shared family delight. Edging the garden and path was a wire fence, at its foot a hawthorn hedge, barely newborn.

Beyond the back garden lay a tract of open ground, muddy and pallid, a winding pavement on its way to town, hugging the houses' back gardens. A huge hump lay against a thick hawthorn hedge shielding a primary school. The Hump, as we called it, was the remnants of the workhouse, now an overgrown lump of broken bricks and stunted grass, nothing grew there. It had an atmosphere all of its own.
We played on it sometimes, rolling and hiding in drier summer months, playing Cowboys and Indians, reenacting the latest film or television series, cowboys always winning. Lee Enfield rifles carved by penknives into discarded lumps of wood or bows and arrows made from sinewy branches. Some Dads reenacted their own childhoods by detailing rifles - smoothing handles, sandpapering barrels and curving triggers. Many battles were fought, won and lost on that humpy hill. No one liked to stay on the mound for too long. It was a chilly place, even on a warm summer's day.

We preferred the long grass, hiding, looking at the clouds swirl slowly overhead, the birds gathered in couples or v-shaped squadrons as we ground-dwellers jealously watched their freedom. Those were the long summer days.

A Bump on the Road

The Hump was now smothered by a white blanket, barely noticeable, above; a white haze hovered, glittering in the weak sun, attempting to drain the chill from the air. Here, stood part of the workhouse, its last addition, where the unfortunate inhabitants were taught sewing, laundry skills or carpentry, depending on their sex. However, not long after this was built, the dilapidated workhouse had completed its life's purpose, and became the local council's store.

One stormy night, the roof disappeared causing the building's demise and the workhouse was stripped of anything useful. It stood empty and barren, a local landmark, providing the path with its name- initially called the Workhouse Path, then the Work Path and finally, the Path. Over the years, the stone walls were tumbled and used for other buildings. During one operation, the basement floor unearthed a darker past - numerous bones. It was rumoured that the manager had housed more occupants than desired, claiming additional funds and hastening the death of the poor unfortunates, their remains buried in the basement cellar. This was the Hump. It was a quiet scandal and, like the workhouse poor, buried quickly. Many locals' relatives unceremoniously became residents and so, by guilt or neglect, the townspeople overlooked the unpleasantness in communal amnesia.

"Are you ready yet?" called my mother. "Come on down for your breakfast."

I scrambled into my brown corduroy trousers, new for Christmas, and taking off my pajama jacket in the unheated bathroom I speedily wiped my face and neck, its window, frosted, inside and out. Wearing my mother-knitted Aran jumper, and after taking two stairs down at a time, I was sitting at the table by the window of the warm back room, in front of the open fire, the only source of heat.

I lifted the corner of the diamond-shaped net curtain, outside the sun cast a pearly shadow over the garden and the sky revealed hints of pale blue. I heard the clink of plates from the kitchen and went out to get my bowl of steaming porridge. Taking it back to the table and placing it on

A Bump on the Road

a table mat of Scottish mountains and flowing streams, I sprinkled sugar across its stagnant top and poured the doorstep-icy creamy topping from the milk, forming a white circle around the edge of the bowl. My plan for eating started there and working inwards, until milk and porridge mixed into a smooth paste, and I spooned it up.

My mother arrived with tea and thickly cut bread. Reaching for the large toasting fork which sat by the fire, she forked the bread into the crust and watched me holding it close to the roasting embers. Within minutes, both sides were browned and I was buttering it thickly.

"Eat up, we'll not be going for a while," said she.

"Can I go out?"

"Just for five minutes. And don't dare get your clothes dirty!"

I scoffed the warm food before dashing to the cupboard under the stairs. There, my duffle coat hung amidst the musky, heavy coats. My welly boots were stuck deep inside - I had to plunge on my hands and knees into the dank air to retrieve them. Just as I placed my hand on the knob of the back door, my mother breathed into my ears;

"Where are your gloves?"

"Dunno."

"Find them; I think they might be on top of the knitting basket, behind the sofa."

The round cane knitting basket with its narrow waist of red and blue beads contained my mother's current knitting project, topped by a cane-saucer lid; in its concave centre lay a corded loop handle. Balls of wool of various sizes and colour, from past projects, littered its bottom. Beside it, stood a much-dented brass vase filled with grey knitting needles of many lengths and thickness, each crowned with a numbered disc or knob. There, of course, on top of the knitting basket, were my

A Bump on the Road

grey knitted gloves. Suitably assembled, I stepped out onto the back door mat, crunching its layer of virgin snow.

I followed the stream of engraved footprints down the Path. At the bottom of our garden, it took a left turn following the edge of houses. I could see someone ahead and disappear into the fog. The sun was shining on the Hump, its rays reflecting off the haze, but I knew it was too weak to shift the white mask.

Little icy wells spread across the lumpy ground and I went in search of more ice-topped pools. I found one, a hard window into the water-filled hollow, and taking off my glove I poked it with my finger. It didn't break, it hurt. At its edge, I repeated my attempt and crashed into the bleak murk. Finding a stick and prodding the ice until it shattered, shards twisted and I plunged my stick into every icy hole I could find.

Running my fingers along the top of the frost laden grass I scooped some of the white stuff and savoured the ice melting on my tongue. The sun's ray fell upon the Hump. Wanting to get my share of its warmth I ran to the sun spot. Sure enough, little rays warmed my face. I surveyed the surrounding landscape - gaunt trees and obscured houses, their white fences bordered the path. I puffed out and saw the cloud form and swirl in front of my nose, breathing in the sharp air and expelling a cloud, again and again.

Suddenly two people came into view, at the corner of my garden. I instantly recognized the swaddling figure, head nodding in conversation with her chatting partner. It was Aunt 'must go' Kate. She wore her caramel winter coat, with brown fur collar and black boots. Around her neck, a mother-knitted green scarf with matching hat.

She passed our house, most days, down the Path to visit her aunt. As always, she met some other traveler and enjoyed their company as they wandered to their respective duties. 'Must go' Kate got the name because she always fled to the toilet upon entering our house, muttering the words 'must go' on her way.

A Bump on the Road

As she busily chatted with her companion, I called to her from the top of the Hump through the smoggy cold, but she continued talking to her companion. I yelled to her again at the top of my voice, repeatedly but still she continued down the path in conversation, taking no notice of me. It would only take a minute to run over and touch her, to be beside her but she didn't take any heed of me. She was so close. Why can't she hear me? I could feel my toes nipping with cold, my legs felt numb, and rooted to the spot.

Someone or something was willing me to stay. Aunt 'must go' Kate was getting away from me, so I dashed off the mound, feeling as if I was ploughing through several feet of snow and yelling her name, she immediately turned to me and looked with amazement into my face. Running and jumping into her arms, I nearly toppled her, her walking companion reaching out to steady her.

"Holy Mary, Mother of God, where were you hiding? Oh, my goodness, what's wrong with ye, you look as you've seen a ghost!"

A Bump on the Road

Our Place

Nothing much happened here. Looking down onto the crescent - its ordinary rows of neatly curtained two-story houses with little sloping gardens walled by hedges and flowers, kids played in the streets and kids and neighbours occasionally had skirmishes, but nothing unusual in that. I lived at the corner end, the exception, and our plot was left to nature, escaping man's attention. Our windows were permanently covered with faded curtains, its occupants permanently ignored, living outside the accepted norm of the street. Next door, Mrs. Samuel, a Protestant, friendly but distant, always on hand as emergencies developed, handing out sympathy and freshly-made chips in newspaper cones. Being a Protestant was an exception too, but she was embraced by one and all, almost overly so.

Behind our hedge lay the decaying, double-fronted, farm house; its sweeping driveway and lawn ran to the road below. It stood beyond a field, the treed border ransacked by countless youths and years of Tarzan-like adventures, ropes hung instead of lianas, weathered and broken tree houses nested precariously amid the upper branches. Our play was tolerated along this demarcation line. Sometimes we ventured beyond and gazed into the darkened interiors, but we withdrew from the forbidden territory at the least suspicion of being caught. Despite the undressed windows, little could be seen.

The interior of our house could not be viewed from without; heavily draped windows blocked the view both ways. Even the frosted bathroom windows were shielded likewise. I often placed myself between the curtains and the glass to look out; many times I stood there unbeknown to family entering the room.

The room within I stood had the barest and neatest necessities for the requirements of slumber and dressing. It had a high metal-spring bed framed by sheets of walnut, a matching dressing table, a huge wardrobe in the corner, and a wood-patterned lino floor, all surrounded by dull wallpaper of small embossed roses. The dominating quilt of lush red roses contrasted with the overall restraint in the furniture and design.

A Bump on the Road

Underneath lay a pale mat easing the feet onto the cool surface, where the Christian family serenely whispered their nightly knelt prayers and centred above the bed - a crucifix. Another small admission to comfort was an upholstered seat in a wickerwork chair by the bed. Visitors to the sick sat here, enhanced by the small fire. A luminescent figure depicting Christ's last hours hung over the fireplace. By day discarded clothing lay askew. Subdued daylight flooded this utilitarian place of rest.

The other two bedrooms were just as stark and mapped out, both contained double beds as the family grew into small people. Less fashionable mismatched furniture lined the wall. Similar twilight fell from the curtained windows. The rooms were always tidy, evidence of daily duties. Atop the stairwell, the bathroom, with matching white ware of the same hue, little open window freshening nature's odours. Broken schisms of soap solidified in the drain wells of the bath while full bars sat on the folded facecloth, its partner draped over the edge of the bath. A frosted window above the sink floods the room, a plastic tumbler with scrappy toothbrushes, flattened by the powered toothpaste which sat alongside. Toiletries line the window sill. Lino flowed out and down the stairs to the kitchen. A favourite game involved sliding down from the turn to the bottom, on each bump gurgling a ba-ba-ba sound; if you were really brave, face downward was the way to go.

The kitchen: painted below and wallpapered above, its jaw box beneath the window witnessed weekly child-baths or the routine of motherly duties. Wooden cabinets lined the wall, a small drop-leaf table underneath, a twin-tub under the stair well and, inside, coats, brushes and other domestic instruments. The fun usually started on wash day, ejecting the wet tangled mass into the spin dryer, patting them down, covering them with its plastic top close the lid and away we go on the vibrator. Hanging off the side, the body pulsated with the orgasmic shudder of the spinning tub; wobbly bits ecstatic - the extent of my excitement.

The two rooms downstairs contrasted in use and design. The living room assembled the family for food, TV and heat. Here we gathered around the open fireplace, always warm and snug, children sat up on the

A Bump on the Road

sofa, Mum and Dad in their chair fireside. Tumbling children rushed from Saturday night baths to be dried and warmed. Dressing gowns lined up. On one particular winter's night a piece of coal shot out igniting me within seconds before being rolled and extinguished by sisterly efforts. We lived, ate and stayed warm in this room.

The good room was at the front, heavily curtained, shadows falling even in the summer. A mystery room, cool and asleep, only to be awakened by a burning fire for the excitement of visitors or Christmas, outside the routine. I seldom sat on the embossed three piece suite or saw the brass animals edging the mantelpiece and the brass candle-sticks acting as sentinels on the hearth. A bookcase stood to the right holding books of various qualities, both in writing and condition, pushed into alignment, a shiny set of new children's encyclopaedia shouldered the other books, never opened, to the left, aglow with shiny ornaments and china tea sets, never used. The door was permanently locked.

Lines of washing were strung along the long thin garden, up-righted with finely planed poles or irregular branches, surprisingly long enough to support the sheets or personal pieces of clothing much sought after by moonlit thieves. The cemented yard, the coal shed led onto the lanky garden of hedges and vegetables. Rows of potatoes, cabbages, and other root veggies fought with the ever-forceful weeds. This Garden of Eden was a contrast to the untamed garden at the front, testament to my father's efforts.

Plenty of green spaces occupied our bit of our world; huge strips of forgotten land lay along the little school behind, falling away to the main road. In the centre lay the green, mainly the domain of the kids who lived at the upper end of the crescent. Here more formal games were played out in seasonal succession; cricket and tennis in summer, soccer all year round.

The imaginary play, seeded by Hollywood or Pinewood, allowed us to travel the imagined worlds of the wild west of America or the wild jungles of Africa or the wild woods of Sherwood Forest. Our neglected fields and trees were the fodder of childhood escape, feeding our

A Bump on the Road

imagination. The real world of family routine interrupted this boy's adventure with mealtime and bedtime. Dirty, damp and cold weather drove us into the living room and the television, a world outlined by countries far away, so removed from our reality, of apartments in big cities, of sun, of adults playing with children, making floral pen containers, and problems solved by worried grown-ups. I didn't have any problems, I wasn't allowed too. Life was ordinary, nothing happened.

I sat on a corner wall half way up the street with a couple of my mates, deciding what to do. Someone wanted to get the ball or head down towards the river for a walk, but nobody was really enthusiastic about anything, just happy to fiddle away the time. In the end, we were still there when John Crossman cycled into our company.

"Well", says he, "have you seen them?"

"Who?" came our reply, totally confused about his ramblings.

"They are up there, some people are just floating about, spinning around, some are grabbing at trees, they couldn't stay upright but they seem to float off again". John told us his Mum had taken him to the head of the town, below Wiry Hill, near the copse of chestnuts, and had seen several of them hanging onto the trees.

We, of course, doubted his tales, and started to heap on the abuse. Pat, an elder boy, pushed John on his shoulder, nearly making him fall off his bike. He had barely said, "Stop winding us up, or I'll thump ya", when along floated a bloke in grey trousers and a yellow spray jacket, nonchalantly waving to us as he disappeared behind a group of houses. He could stay upright; perhaps he had some astronaut training. We looked at each other, almost going red with the embarrassment of not knowing how to react. We set off looking for more evidence of this weird event. It wasn't long before we saw another one floating above a house. It was the talk on every one's lips. Within days, other news interspersed with the 'Floaters'.

A Bump on the Road

As the days of the summer and holidays wore to a close, more and more people were floating above the houses and countryside. Amazingly earth-bound people adapted to seeing oscillating humans perform stunts only seen in the circus. On the serious side, some parents organised clothing, shelter, and food; fish and chips seemed to be the favourite. They were placed on platforms in the branches. John said he could smell the vinegar. Many of these platforms were built on trees and tall buildings where family and friends could leave food and clothing. Some tried to capture them and place the people in cages or houses, but every time this was attempted the Floaters' restlessness became intolerable and peace could only be achieved by releasing them into the open again. Some were given sleeping tablets or injections, but after they woke they became physically uncontrollable. As the trees were losing their leaves, some found shelter in church steeples and belfries, which soon became places of refuge and food. They could not settle in one place and moved on after a time. The Floaters had problems when they wanted to empty themselves. Piddling from a height wasn't any problem unless someone was caught underneath the stream, but excreting proved a slightly bigger challenge. They could land and use ordinary toilets but tended to float above and sometimes missed. It required a deft feat of manoeuvring. Within weeks specially designed privies were built by councils and parishes. The structures were positioned inside bell towers, on the sides of buildings, and up trees.

So who were these Floaters? People were worried that they might be the next to float, but as it turned out the Floaters were all violent people. Anyone who had used violence: the Irish Republican Army, the Ulster Volunteer Force, and the myriad in between, bank robbers, even some people who had no connection to gangs would appear floating about, but they soon disappeared again. Indeed, I saw one of my neighbours, a big bad-tempered bloke who routinely struck out at anything in his path floating along one day. The last I heard of him, he had floated off to England.

For months, the issue was much discussed on TV, on the radio, in the newspapers, on the street corner, in the home, from the pulpit. How would the country cope with this phenomenon? With Christmas

A Bump on the Road

coming, wide-spread discussion centred on how we could help the people doomed to float. Did they deserve their destiny? Life in the towns and countryside settled into a peaceful routine, with the newfound absence of violence, as all the perpetrators had transcended above. I was in my friend's house having tea when a news report came on that someone had been arrested by police for shooting at the Floaters. Two had been found dead, caught in trees in Hammersmith, London. A group of Floaters had armed themselves. Where they'd gotten the guns, no one knew.

It was Sunday morning and I was once again sitting on the kerb outside the house, waiting for my parents. We were off to church this time. Birds flew in triangular squadrons to the copse in the field. Some families were going to the same church and were setting out to walk, saying hello as they passed. We were going in the car. Many curtains were still drawn. Many residents were still in bed on this cool ashen morning.

As we clamoured out of the car in the church car park, I met Tom, my mate. I asked my Mum could I sit with Tom but she said no, we had to go to visit Granny, as we did every weekend. I promised Tom we would go out on the bikes to see some Floaters after my visit to Granny, if it stayed dry.

"What? What are Floaters?" Tom asked with a puzzled expression. "What do you mean?" I responded. "The people floating about in the sky! It was all so peaceful until yesterday. Are you pulling my leg?"

Tom burst out laughing, gazing at me as if I was mad. My mother shot me a dirty look as we entered the church and dragged our family in the opposite direction to Tom's. Back to boring normality, I suppose, but it seemed so real.

A Bump on the Road

The Front Row

The Front Row had bigger gardens and facades. All were semi-detached with concrete lintels over the windows and pillared porches embossing the front doors. Concrete walls bordered the neat gardens, each wall topped with iron railings. Initially the tenants were carefully selected to ensure they appreciated the extra features. The houses were grander, the occupants posher. Between the main road and the Front Row lay a green swathe of mostly low bushes and a few trees. This was the view often seen by the travelling public as they passed along to their destinations: clipped hedges, mowed lawns, borders of perennial planting, a row of cultivated living and trimming. The smell of mown grass wafted on soft balmy summer evenings.

Their back gardens were an industry of burgeoning greenery, producing edible fare for each season. Windowed sheds harboured meticulously maintained tools; projects of construction and often repair. These sheds were bastions of D.I.Y. for the male refugee seeking asylum from work and family, spending his free time working on projects that never seem to get finished. Little seats made of cushioned bags sat in the corner; hidden sacks of tobacco close to hand, even the odd beer could be stowed away from prying eyes. Tools were forbidden playthings.

Indeed the shed was out of bounds most of the time, except during the long damp school holidays, when frustrated mothers needed a space for their offspring to while away their free time, out of the cool rainy elements, but more importantly out of their sight. The shed became more than a workshop - it became living space, away from the home. One enthusiastic father installed a stove that sent a trail of smoke over the other backyards, its chimney too low to allow escape, sending sooty debris into the newly laundered clothing and bedding hung on the long lines of personal paraphernalia.

A Bump on the Road

The stove in the shed belonged to the first house of the Front Row. A pebble-dashed gable wall and a garden wall stretched from the front to the lane at the back of the house, blocking the view of the back garden and shed. The black pipe of a chimney on the shed stood above the garden wall. The gable wall was fronted by a small narrow path, terminating at a gated entry to the back. This was the biggest house in the Front Row. Next door lived Captain O'Neill.

Captain O' Neil's son, Liam was my age, went to the same school as I did, and I guess we grew up together, except that he grew faster than me, so while we may have grown up together, he was always a head above, not only above but sideways too. He grew outward, probably to the size of someone twice his age, really useful, as no one messed him around, so no one messed with me either. This did not include adults. I may have been threatened, given the eye and dirty vengeful looks, but given I was in his mate, I was mostly left alone. Several moments of panic I remember vividly, when caught alone. However, despite these stomach churning incidents, I seem to have come through unscathed.

Liam was sometimes called Captain too. Liam's father was named because he was away at sea most of the time, home for a few months, sometimes weeks, and then off again. Captain resented the absent father, although he never said so, but told me tales his father had told him of derring-do in foreign fields and ports: finding gold in Australia, escaping pirates in the Caribbean or finding oil in Texas. His father's stories often coincided with recent films on the television. Captain O'Neil actually spent most of his time riding the waves of the Irish Sea, so, most of the time; the exotic ports were Belfast and Liverpool. However, over the years he took different positions that allowed him to visit many ports all over the world.

Young Captain had a bedroom facing the main road. He was lucky; his older brothers had left home and were working in England, and a sister was still at home, completing her final examinations at school. She was the first O'Neil that would go to university - a studious, quiet girl who never give young Captain much trouble, just reminding him to do his chores and homework, but helpful in both.

A Bump on the Road

His bedroom consisted of a double bed, a wooden, leather-seated dining chair from his Gran's, a chest of drawers, darkened by age, a built-in wardrobe that frequently took him on his own adventures over the seas, and walls of tiny flowers that he never really noticed. The window was draped in thick green, the net curtains providing privacy and softness, often stuck to the window on sharp frozen nights. His only form of heat at night was a hot water bottle and layers of blankets. Money was not a problem in this household. His father had regular employment and the boys sent money and presents home.

Captain had a bird's eye view of the passing world from his window: a bus stop opposite, a side road where cars could pull in and where people, mostly men, got lifts. Few had cars, people took buses or walked. To his right, a cul-de-sac provided a turning area and was treed, sheltered from the main road and the housing nearby, a perfect place for awkward courting couples to share furtive kisses. The main road led over the bridge and into the town or onto the next village. This passing parade of people and vehicles was a slight distraction for Captain and me on a wet weekend or on long dull grey summer holidays. During the summer, we'd watch marching parades, various community groups or bands striding up and down the Main Road, anything to distract us for a few minutes from our usual routine. Sometimes, we watched from the bedroom, other times we stood by the kerb staring at gaily coloured uniforms and listening to their music.

On occasion I slept over with Captain during the holidays. We would watch through the window, and see the cars and lorries flow in both directions. One Saturday night after midnight, when everyone had gone to bed, we knelt up, cloaked in the curtain looking out. It was a mild clear night, and Saturday was always a sure bet to watch the couples swooning in the car below.

"Wouldn't it be great if we could hitch a ride to the seaside or a big city, or surprise me Da in some port, just walk up to him and say, 'How's it going, Da?'" said Captain.

A Bump on the Road

"Yeah. Sitting up in those high cabs, looking down, watching everything go by, and just travelling on. It would be great to drive one of those big things. Did you see that one? It had two sets of back wheels. What was it carrying?" I asked.

"Don't know, going far too fast," replied Captain.

Just then a car pulled into the cul-de-sac, and into the little turning area sheltered from passing cars and eyes. The inside light flickered, illuminating two animated faces, and then blinked off again. The two melted into one. Screeching brakes tore our eyes to the main road as a cab with a trailer pulled up. The driver got out, lifted something from the front of the cab, put it on the pavement, looked around, climbed back in and screeched off in a hiss of a second. The car couple couldn't see what had happened as they were out of sight of the road.

"What is it?"

"Your guess is as good as mine," said Captain, looked at me.

The clock struck one and both of us looked at it simultaneously. Our eyes met, we smiled and after a few silent moments we were turning the back door key. With a clunk, it opened. Stepping outside together, our bare feet cut into the iron grill for cleaning muddy boots.

"Daaa-ump", muttered Captain, as he muffled his agony. A similar utterance from me had us grabbing each other to silence and support our fumbling exit. We walked slowly to the shed, taking large steps and glanced in the moon light at our red and tracked feet, realising the back door was still open. Captain went back, as agile as possible, to gently close it and then returned.

"What now?" says Captain, wishing he had stayed in bed.

"We could go in our bare feet, its dry tonight," said I.

A Bump on the Road

"My bloody foot is sore, I think it's bleeding. My welly boots are in the shed, is it open?"

The worn handle turned easily, and pushing the door open I stepped into the blackness. After a moment I stuck my head out again.

"Too dark, do you know where they are?"

"Yeah, let me go in", he whimpered.

"'Sore?"

"Too bloody right! Christ, my head! Bloody rake; it's never usually there!"

"Go on your hands and knees," I whispered.

Gently, he tossed out some boots. I found a pair that fitted, and put them on. Captain emerged from the shed.

"Those are my boots, get them off!"

Seeing the red vertical indent on his forehead, I didn't argue. I found a pair that made me wobble a bit as I walked but at least my feet were covered.

"Right, let's go," whispered Captain, subduing his pain and regaining enthusiasm for our night adventure. We left the garden, and brushing along the garden hedges, we emerged from the lane at the other end of the Front Row. No one was about. The bright moon gave plenty of light, the weather was cool but pleasant; cars and lorries rolled along on the main road. We crossed onto the grass verge that separated our road from the main one. On this side no bushes provided cover, so the couple in the car could have seen us. Bending as low as possible, and moving as fast as my welly boots allowed, we looked on the pavement for what the driver had thrown. There it laid, a dead cat; he had run over a cat. We ran across to the bushes on our side, penetrating the

A Bump on the Road

undergrowth to get out of sight. The rhododendron bushes provided a hollow centre down the verge, to the parked car. We rarely played here, a green island beside a busy and noisy thoroughfare. The leaves provided cover but also prevented us from seeing into the car. However, we could hear low voices and jostling sounds.

As Captain tried to peak through the green curtain, the car started up and he fell back onto a protruding branch.

"Shit!"

"Shush, they are driving away. They probably saw your ugly mug and it scared the bejasus out of them," I laughed.

Captain was not for laughing! Rubbing his rump, he made off across the road and fled into the shelter of the lane. Suddenly, I could hear the strains of a marching band in the distance. Within seconds it was on the road beside me. I crawled under the bush and looked in awe as the marchers strode solemnly in time to the music, their flutes horizontal against their mouths, the melody flowing on the air above their lips, weaving between the band members and balancing over the Lambeg Drum at the rear, whose player tapped, tapped with insistent force upon the skin. Slowly they glided into the night, moving in step, their red brocade fading into the still air. I stood up, dumb-founded. What was that at this hour of the night?

I turned and skeltered to the lane, turning back to look at the road, the intermittent traffic droning to their journey's end. Captain was nowhere to be seen. I stepped as quiet as my boots allowed, opened the gate and there he was, standing expectantly on the doorstep, signalling me to enter. He ushered me in, his finger over his lips. We dropped the boots outside and after locking the door, we crept up the carpeted stairs. Inside the bedroom, I said,

"Did you see that? The.. the band?"

"Go to sleep, shush."

A Bump on the Road

"Did you see them?"

"Go to sleep."

Did Captain see them too and could not believe his eyes? Was he as confused as me?

I couldn't sleep for a good ten minutes.

A Bump on the Road

Family Secret

Memories are notoriously dodgy. Childhood memories are no different, often formed in moments of heightened enjoyment and sadness, or simply in expectation of Christmas, birthdays, holidays or the steamy atmosphere of the kitchen emitting the smell of a stew on a cold damp winter's day. Being thrashed, or the threat of being thrashed, swung the pendulum of emotions. The routine of daily life at home and at school is barely recalled, stored in the deep, deep recesses of our brains, neither traumatised by injury nor clouded in the wistful whisperings of childhood days. First memories are strangest of all, billowing clouds of good times, unpleasant bits and pieces ignored. These are my memories, my story, and my life.

My first memory is the clothesline stretching from one end of the long, narrow back garden to the other, meeting in a point. A pole or two supported the clothesline. Later I was to ride in my imagination and charge the infidels using the pole as a lance, in my role as a crusading Christian knight serving God and country. Prior to using this pole for support the washing on the line, we washed the family's necessities in the twin tub, its vibrating necessitating the empting of my bladder. A similar wobble was brought on by lying down and sliding down the stairs.

After the garments swished and swung, the water darkening to a dull grey, the timer pinged and they were pulled into the spin drier, damp and twisted. Sometimes it became unbalanced, at this point the operator needs to free the offending items and extract the liquid. After each spin the clothes were carried to the outside line for drying and freshened in the cool northerly wind.

Running through the sheets and clothes and other personal items was a weekly routine. Often we would play by racing through them, pulling them off their pegs and falling onto the ground, our antics answered by a thump at the window from within ordering us to lower the pole and re-hang the items. Clothes were brought in before nightfall as we had our fair share of spiders and earwigs in the house already. A more mysterious hazard, the knickers thief, was fodder for neighbours' gossip.

Many homes had a good room at the front, a dusky mottled place with a heavily laced window, housing a three-piece sculptured suite, a glass cabinet displaying wedding present china, ornaments of various hues and a dead fireplace - lit on holidays, special occasions or for visitors. To the rear, a small working kitchen and pantry wallpapered with kitchen implements. A gas cooker and jaw box in constant use, as was the back sitting room, with fire, light and family. The TV room was perennially filled with news, films and favourite children's programs: swashbuckling yarns of derring-dos, goodies versus baddies, war movies, cowboys and Indians. The good guys, the omnipresent John Wayne, tough on the outside, heart of gold on the inside, never the oppressor. British movies were dismissed as inferior to the high budget Hollywood dramas of the Wild West. British characters were easy to spot; the working class spiv, the jolly hockey sticks brigade, the stiff upper lipped, the anally retentive or the war hero. In this room the family ate and socialised, children sent out to play on good days and sometimes even on not so good days.

This was an era of children amusing themselves, finding friends on the street, the next-door neighbour, playing in the surrounding fields and streets. Parents did not entertain their offspring or ensure they had energetic leisure pursuits or educational and arty pursuits. Children did play the piano, join choirs or dance a jig but mostly were left to organise their free time as they pleased. Amusements were found in the street with mates, home-made wooden gun, bows fashioned from apple saplings and arrows peeled back to the moist green bark, the raw smoothness unpleasant to touch, finding youthful skin to jab. Girls did other things with dolls. Slingshots were common, but banned from our house, the potential for damage too great. Their design and manufacture were stunning, cut from tyres or rubber tubes, the Y-shaped holder carved with care and worn with use, slugging birds out of the sky and no doubt smashing windows.

A Bump on the Road

Memories are notoriously dodgy. My childhood seemed pleasant and normal. All families are unique and yet the same, ours was no exception. We learned to live and play in a kind of harmony and to share the load of our collective secrets – their existence imperceptibly arriving on our consciousness – unaware that neighbours were similarly engaged. Had the secrets been given light, they would have evaporated and changed us forever. It was not the secrets themselves, but the manner in which we dealt with them that ultimately formed us.

The process of guarding secrets began at an early age. The first of our family's secrets was that nobody must ever go upstairs. I don't remember the rule being spelt out to me, but I became aware of it when visiting my friend Mary's house. Her bedroom was very different from the one I shared at home. Some of the less appealing characteristics of our bedroom could be pinpointed without much effort – the offender: the coats on the bed. We had what my mother referred to as 'fine, warm army coats' on every bed in the house. Mary had a pink eiderdown and it looked light and beautiful. How could I ever live down the disgrace of her knowing that we lay under those huge monstrosities every night? I imagined many of my other pals had lovely bedrooms. I was so busy making sure nobody stumbled on our shame that I didn't realise that I never got to their inner sanctums. It was only in later years we discovered that many families had beds bedecked with army coats! But there were many years of 'close shaves', as Mary or other pals suggested some game or other to be played 'up your stairs'.

Our Granny had always lived with us; I was eight when she died. The only feelings I can recall were a mixture of panic, irritation and delight. The delight was due to the fact that I could now invite friends to our house to play upstairs, where Granny's bedroom had been. "Our Granny's very old and sick," we used to say. "She can't talk except to say 'Josie,' our Mum's name, and she cries all the time. She can't get out of bed, either, or go to the lav, so she has to have nappies." My accompanying wriggle of the nose and rolling of eyes indicated what a cross this was to bear and explained away, at a stroke, why there were any offensive odours and why access to our upstairs was difficult. What kid would want to risk being caught while running past this odd creature? The irritation arose from what I perceived to be a lack of fuss or pity from others at my great loss when she died. After all, I'd just lost a grandmother! But nobody seemed to think this was tragic and my mother appeared to be the only one to illicit much sympathy from people. I was resentful that at school I wasn't even allowed to stay inside for the day – a concession usually given by the teacher when some significant event, like a new baby or sick parent or death, occurred in the family. I tried to feign sorrow by mimicking the sad faces of my two older sisters in an effort to squeeze some show of sympathy from someone – anyone – but I eventually accepted that my delight at having no more smells upstairs, like all my pals, was stronger than my other feelings. And somehow it seemed adults could detect those feelings, no matter how careful you were to hide them.

Another of our dark secrets surfaced at this time. My parents, being 'blow-ins', had only lived in the town for about 10 years. Granny was to be buried over 40 miles away. Neighbours asked if she was to be buried with her husband. This was met by my mother muttering something and going off into another dramatic fit of crying. If the neighbours didn't smell a rat, we children did. One of us would pose a question like, "When did Granda die?" and our mother would tell us that we were 'ould hens', or some such pejorative creature, and not to ask that question again. We knew enough from the tone of her voice to never attempt to do so. But it gave us a topic for hushed bedtime conversations under the army coats.

"Wonder whatever happened to Grandad?"

Christy could always be relied upon to come up with the juiciest answer.

"Probably Granny murdered him before she left Galway."

Although we all immediately protested, we all considered it a real possibility. In fact, as far as I was concerned, it fed our wish for more drama in our lives. There was definitely something mysterious about our grandfather. After all, why was it none of us talked about him?

A Bump on the Road

It was now our shared mission to ensure no-one ever suspected the truth, whatever that might be. The only thing that was certain was that it wasn't something good; otherwise, we knew our mother would be glad to tell people. For the foreseeable future, all talk about grandparents was off the agenda. And if ever anyone brought up the subject of Grandad with Mammy, whichever child was present would immediately interrupt, often in the most dramatic of ways.

Memories are notoriously dodgy but memories and secrets - a lethal combination. The more secrets there were, the more resourceful we were in making up excuses. Was it family loyalty or just vanity? Did we have a family secret? Who knows? All I know is, we sure as hell didn't want to be found out.

A Bump on the Road

Run

They came at us from the back lanes, spilling through the trees. How they managed to surprise us without our scouts seeing them we'll never know, unless our scouts were traitors or had been captured. We held our positions momentarily, but the hail of small stones from the tree tops sent us scurrying into the centre of the crescent, only to be attacked from there too. There must have been thirty of them. This part of the street was dangerous for me; it was too close to home.

The surprise attack was too soon, too quick for us, we were not ready. More seemed to pour from the side road and completely surround us. Our natural reaction would usually be surrender. Yet for some reason, yelling with fear, perhaps initiated by our leader, Lanky, we charged through the smallest engagement of the enemy towards the upper end of the street and thankfully away from my house.

Crunches of wood on wood and wood on legs and arms, thuds and yelps shot through the air. As we ran, the screams of success from the enemy hordes behind us sounded too close. We splintered in all directions. I ran with my partner Deccy and two others up the back alley of some houses in the next street. Looking behind from a safe distance, we could see the stunned faces of the Tinnies, our boyhood enemies from the bungalows a few streets away. Their brilliant plan had surprisingly failed to capture us and our equally surprising escape had caused disarray in all our ranks.

"Jesus, did you see that? How the hell did it happen?"

"Dunno", said James, "but I got bloody thumped on me legs."

"Quick, in here. They are starting to search for us," I said.

"Shit, into the shed quick," said Deccy.

The Tinnies seemed to have reorganised and split into groups: a few after us, and the others chasing the rest of our group who had scattered

A Bump on the Road

towards the main road. With any luck they would find their way home. We slipped through the hedge bordering the garden and opened the shed door, unsure of what we would find, hoping not to find a sleeping dog. Nothing, only darkness. I held the door closed from within, silence, listening intently as the gang swept by, running up the alley past our refuge. Hearing their squeals we stood still for a few minutes, holding our breaths.

"Are they gone?"

"Think so!"

I listened as hard as possible, hearing the dog bark next door when he heard us move. Pushing the door open slowly, I listened again, then stepped gingerly to the garden gate and peered over it - all clear. I ran back to the shed, shutting the door immediately. We stood, holding our breath again, listening, and started to relax.

James farted in the darkness, so we swept out to bright, cool air, laughing with hands over our mouths, but tumbled behind the hedge immediately, again listening, terrified, as we heard some shouts. They must be close by, somewhere.

Thankfully, there was no one in the house looking out onto the garden. If there had been; they would have seen four bare-legged boys lying on their stomachs, craning their necks through the bottom of the hedge to scan the lane.

"We'll split up", says James, farting again, "I need to go to the loo, I need to go home. I'm heading back the way we came. Comin' Deccy? What about you, Johno?"

"Aye, awright," they both answered.

"I'll head up the ways, meself, might be better on my own anyway. I think they are down at the bottom still. You can head back but I am headin' up cause I think they'll all be there waitin' for us to return."

A Bump on the Road

"Jasus, I can't wait, I'll wet myself," says James.

Off they went down the alley, keeping close to the fences and each other, leaving me crouched in the hedgerow amid nettles and rat holes. I watched as they crossed the bottom of the alley, darting into oblivion. What now?

Strategy, as Lanky O'Neill, our leader, kept reminding us, is key to any battle. Having studied numerous army picture comics, he told us he was aware of all the techniques of warfare known to all the great generals.

Our side comprised of a motley crew, all shapes, sizes and ages. Some wore green as Lanky had decreed green was our colour. Our forward attack group was known as the Giants, led by Lanky himself, this taller group giving cover for our smaller group to cut and thrust from behind and in between. His tactical exhortation was: work in pairs. Sure enough, it had paid off in two previous skirmishes, preventing capture and serious hurt.

My partner, Deccy, had prevented our capture on both occasions by the well known strategy known as 'Run'. At one point, when we seemed to be stranded and at risk of capture, Deccy roared at me, 'Run'. It worked.

Our armoury comprised of spears, shields and swords, similar in style to our enemy but not in colour. We were in various shades of green; the enemy were mostly in red. I had my personal handmade sword and shield, carefully pared with knives and chisels. All had been secretly made in my father's shed, the finishing touches carved meticulously for days with an old penknife from my Uncle Jimmy. I was particularly proud of my heart shaped shield emboldened with a Celtic cross, now a legendary survivor of the two previous engagements with the Tinnies.

However, we did not have a name and, despite numerous discussions, it had never been finalised. My suggestion was The Crescent Warriors. Today's fateful battle marked a turning point in the ongoing summer holiday skirmishes; the last major entanglement.

A Bump on the Road

How do I get home? Deccy and the other two did not come back past me, had they been captured or did they make it back home? I thought I would travel up the alley and, if stuck, could take shelter in a mate's house up there. I could always jump a hedge, and hide in a back garden again, if necessary, but being caught by an adult who might tell my parents could be worse than being caught by the Tinnies.

At the top of the back lane I could wait until the coast was clear and run into the next alley and then down into our street, with cover all the way. Most back gardens had hedges blocking the rear view of the houses, with gates leading up the paths to the back door. Often they were painted green, adding another shade of emerald in their moist gardens. Some had thriving vegetable plots, others were neglected and weedy, a muddy dog pen with a kennel here and there, the back door often scratched by the animal, wanting social warmth.

I made it to the top without any hassle, glanced out from the hedge-filled edge, and spotted several of the enemy sitting on a foot-high wall facing away their headquarters, a horse box with its ramp down. Inside I saw a table and darkened shapes milling around. I pulled back and waited.

Looking out again after a minute, the same scene greeted me. I could make a dash down the open road and, if spotted by the trio on the wall, I might be able to outrun them as I had a good start. Providing I didn't run into any others, coming up.

It was also possible that the Tinnies wouldn't rough me up in such an open space, with the possibility of been seen by adults. I reckoned this was my best bet, the best strategy of them all – Run. I retreated again into the long grass under the hedge, waiting for the right moment. Listened intently, crouching on all fours and wishing I had vertical dog ears. Again I went forward, the same scene; nothing to my right, the road was empty. I could do it. Moving on all fours to the road I stood up, ready to run.

A Bump on the Road

I was immediately grabbed from behind, arms twisted up my back, kneed in the bottom of my spine. Forcibly stooped, I was frog-marched to their headquarters. The two boys who had captured me had swollen expressions of laughter, hooting to the three on the wall, who jumped, whooping, from their seats, waving their swords and shields in victory.

Fear and tears welled inside me, as I was pushed up the ramp and into the trailer. The ramp was pulled closed. The joyous bellowing stopped as I was stood in front of a table with the scent of horse manure up my nose and fear in my belly. The older boy behind the table, sitting on a box, has glee written all over his face. His cheeks were risen red, his eyes wide open, his mouth half smiling, relishing his moment of power. He leaned forward.

"Name," he shouted, I gave it.

"Are you a spy? Are you a sss...spy?" he yelled into my ear.

He repeated, shouting as loud as he could. Terror was his game, and he worked it into a frenzy. The rest joined him in a chorus of 'we kill spies; we kill spies,' while banging the sides of the horse trailer. I was terrified.

They ripped my T-shirt and vest off over my head. God, I thought, they are going to strip me. Beating me up would be less embarrassing. Being stripped was just too much; my legs became jelly, their excited faces, a reddening blur. Bodily functions were committed behind locked bathroom doors, getting ready for bed involved speedy covering of body with pyjamas. Nakedness was not part of my upbringing, nakedness I could not handle. The shame it carried was bottomless. I was on verge of inconsolable tears. Their leader then poked me with his sword and flung my T-shirt at me. I stood upright, surprisingly controlling my fear.

"Put it over your head. Where are the weapons hidden? We want them."

"They got lost," I stammered.

A Bump on the Road

Actually, I hadn't a clue what he was saying. The thought occurred to me, though, that I could use this idea as a bargaining tool. Perhaps they would let me go in exchange for information. I, too, watched spy movies.

"Someone's coming!" one of the boys shouted outside.

With that exclamation, everyone said "Shhh." A sword was pushed into my neck; it was the other enemy, the enemy of the enemy, and they belted the side of the horse box and roared:

"Get out to hell of that box. Get out, and I don't want to see any of yous in there again. Out now!"

The enemy of the enemy is our enemy too, adults, although in this case, the enemy became my saviour. I was glad to see the glowering face of the man as the gate was lowered. My instinct told me to run. I did, and was gone down the street that ran parallel to my street.

"Hey, where are you going? Right all of yous, now not a word from any of yous, put those sticks away and go home too or else I'll tell your parents."

Not looking back once, I pulled on my tops mid-run. I was never so glad to see my house.

It was too late. News of the battles travelled far and wide, the enemy with real power had been alerted and adults roamed the streets mopping up strays with belts across ears and bellows of further retribution.

I was met with parental consternation and sent to my bedroom. After a while, I sneaked into my parents' room to look out their window onto the street. I saw the dregs of warriors scampering for cover or being routed by parents. The sight was depressing: parents walking up and down the pavements or knotted in groups, heads wagging. They had

A Bump on the Road

taken over our streets. My comrades, heads slumped, dragged themselves towards their homes.

Lanky O Neil stood solemnly beneath my window, his father by his side, chatting to my father, their bodies in knowing empathy reflecting each others' gesticulations. Such is the reduced circumstances of a gallant warrior class subdued by a mightier force. Perhaps he saw the curtain move, as Lanky glanced up towards me and, barely moving his head, he winked. It was as good as being knighted. I felt all my soldierly efforts had been worthwhile, and a huge blush rose from my stomach into my face. I floated momentarily. Within minutes, the street was empty.

Mr O'Shea came out of his front door, scanned the street, pulled a weed in his stride to his front hedge and started clipping his privet. Mrs Duncan came round the corner and waddled across the road, towards the town's bridge, shopping bag swinging from one hand. Normality; people going about their chores, but this was the summer and the streets should have been full of school holiday kids amusing themselves under the grey laden sky.

Was this the end of my street-fighting career? Had I received a badge of honour from my leader? I was one of the boys. Being an old hand with three engagements behind me, this was a waste of my talent. I excelled at the cut and thrust of swordplay, and, despite my minor stature, or perhaps because of it, I could sail into the throng and exact some damage. Being an ardent student of Robin Hood, and the swashbuckling Saturday movie matinees, I perfected my skills.

The days of street battles were over. Parents became aware of what had been happening during the long absences of their dear little ones. Strict instructions were laid and retribution was to be swift and severe if caught fighting in the streets again. Fashioning swords and shields in the sheds and garages on rainy days were prohibited, and indeed, any form of woodwork scrutinised.

A Bump on the Road

We were bored kids during these uneventful childhood summers, finding amusement in the soft weather on the damp narrow streets. The fights had never been serious, but we did get bruised and hurt and were fearful of being caught in the enemy territory. Parents didn't think that raging groups of children would hack bits of flesh off each other. They didn't worry that the multitude of kids that swarmed over the pavements, streets and green boggy fields would get into any bother.

Most of our houses looked the same: semi-detached, brick-built and pebble-dashed, metal windows clothed in lace and net, tidy front gardens, green-bordered with privet hedges. Some had narrow back gardens where clothes were hung on long lines to dry. The washing lines were often items of pride; many were creatively constructed, hooked to trees. The longer the better, more room for sheets and clothes. Personal items were hung close to the back yard, out of sight of the knicker-thieves. Wooden or metal posts supported the long lines in the middle. Naturally created wooden hooks where branches divided were sought after and considered lucky. We commandeered some of these poles to be used as lances on the battle field.

There were plenty of adults around to police our streets: many wives stayed at home, and unemployed men occupied their days with their pigeons or racing dogs. They pottered about their sheds and vegetable plots, when not walking to the town, to back a horse; they congregated with their cronies on the street corners to discuss the fate of their losing horses and football teams, or the current state of world affairs. Getting a bat on the head or scolded from some neighbour or adult for misbehaving or for wandering the streets of the town when the children should have stayed closer to home was commonplace. Sometimes meeting an uncle or another relative proved beneficial when a winning horse had provided good form and some cash; a few pennies could send a kid merrily to the first sweetie shop.

Despite dire warnings, the final battle that summer took place at the foot of the hill, every one sworn to secrecy. The hill was a few fields away from our houses, belonging to the Big House, pretty useless and strewn with thistles. It was reputed to be haunted, a burial ground of a

A Bump on the Road

fierce battle between two tribes of Ulster, centuries ago. Previous owners had dug it up and found bones below the surface, so it had been left to Mother Nature. At night people avoided the area and its ghost-stories were well-known, but others dismissed them as the wind in the trees or a trick of light.

In one corner, a grassy knoll separated itself from the rest of the field. Here, another battle was arranged with the Tinnes, only this time, it would be between the big boys. That left me and Deccy out. The open street battles were over but the grassy knoll was hidden from prying adult eyes!

It was to take place at around one in the afternoon in the last week of the holidays on a typically damp, overcast day. We gathered along the hedgerow and kept our distance from the Tinnes. The younger ones like me climbed the trees, to get a better view. There was much talk of an escape route, so we didn't go too high up for fear of capture.

As our crowd was gathering, by the hedge fence, we could see Tinnes gather on the far corner, near the grassy knoll. Deccy and I were up a tree and he called to me to look at what they are carrying, looks like poles, I said. Some poles had flags flying from the top. About a dozen boys were gathering around the knoll and I counted 6 poles, four with flags, red triangles and rectangles. Our boys had nothing like that, and serious discussion ensued. What would they do to oppose such a display of force? Before long all of our force was atop the trees viewing the enemy.

The decision came quickly. The Tinnes formed in a line on the knoll and, holding their lances horizontal, they suddenly charged towards us. Bodies dropped from the trees like apples in the wind. Dull thuds as boys landed on their feet, bums and heads. All ran down the field towards the exit, the gate, the only escape route. More bodies threw themselves over and through the three bar gate, heading down through a wheat field. By our good fortune, getting the lances over the gate slowed the Tinnes and once again we celebrated our luck by utilising

A Bump on the Road

that tried-and-tested strategy, well known to all armies since time began - Run.

A Bump on the Road

Guinness of my Childhood

We lived in The Chalet. It was known locally as The Chalet. It had a huge garden with flower-beds of various hues, and straight-edged lawns with high privet hedges. In the rear garden, paths were laid out in geometric conformity complementing the rows of potatoes, cabbage and runner beans, the green foliage broken by a high-rise of sweet pea. In this ordered garden, policed by my mother, grew a disorderly weeping willow. Despite numerous ties, which would have impressed any hardened scoutmaster, this tree refused to fall and trail as desired. Years of twine hammered into the lawns and walls produced a tree of wilful spite. It entangled the cypress, grew over the wall and most certainly did not provide a veil for the awkward marriage of privet and pebble-dashed wall. It stayed because it was the first planted and, like the first born, it could do no wrong.

Access to The Chalet was by a set of six-foot wrought iron gates: white spirals and black verticals, painted every seventeenth of March, weather permitting. Dad painted these as Mum pruned the ever-increasing varieties of roses and planted some root crops. In the afternoon we set off for the local trots, St. Patrick's Day Races, a favourite of mine. Viewed from the front, our house looked impressive - the added porch built by Dad gave an air of substance.

The private residence sat in the middle of a public housing estate, a place apart, shielded by high hedges; a fortress from without and within. At the windowless side, piles of wood and planks were stacked along a fence, providing a secure parapet to survey the locals. The entire estate was viewed from behind a clematis-covered trellis. Beyond these gates, life, real life, took place - away from the security of privet hedges and warm steamy kitchens. Our street was dominated by The Factory. In a town of high unemployment, it provided the majority of work for men, boys and girls but mostly for women. I walked daily past its huge, noisy security gates; lorries shunting, blue-frocked men jumping from cabs, shouting greetings to the friendly gate men, lazily sauntering to check the documents, payroll security vans whizzing through, alert eyes, stiff countenances, uncomfortable.

A Bump on the Road

Going to the shop one early morning, I discovered a security van's windscreen smashed, glass mosaics scattered on pavement and bonnet. Men in uniform swarmed around, inspecting, measuring, nodding, some curiously laughing, others directing traffic, the vehicle's front wheels half on pavement and kerb. Excitement flooded within as I looked on, real life impinging on school-a-day routine, cops and robbers at last. I moved closer to the van sighting the driver's seat blotted with blood. Too real, too close, perhaps. Just then a flash and two days later me and my two-tone, brown and beige cardigan fronted not just the local paper, but a national daily. Real life, I loved it. A small boy in a small town at the centre of a big story.

Further out onto the Main Road, a different world unfolded, ranging from public housing and factories to imposing detached houses. One in particular, with its English biscuit-box architecture and mopping thatched roof, emphasised another country, another village silhouetted by trees: a posh village with wide roads and traffic travelling to important places, something distinctive from home and inbred culture. The possibility of a life on the periphery, at odds from my own, positioned itself.

Smells and scented atmospheres rekindle memories, transporting me instantly to childhood where the sun was always shining. Several of these moments, intense passages of repeated habits, are exhausting. The smell of a local bakery fills me with promise still and stirs up that life on the edge. That village had an odour, not of weeping conifers, but freshly-baked bread.

One other smell envelops my senses with apprehension and joy, but quite draining. Custard. Many a child remembers custard, but this was School Custard and, no, it was not yellow porridge, lumpy and highland-bracing, the yellow peril, but thin, smooth, flowing, the Guinness of my childhood. My teacher encouraged me to eat it. My reward was tea and biscuits in the classroom. I was a sickly child.

A Bump on the Road

How this situation arose I did not know then, but just took it for granted. I imagine my mother, almost in tears, voice croaking, "It's all very well teaching him his letters and numbers but if he's not fed well up he'll not make it to Dick and Dora!" Food was a bit of a burden during my childhood and primary school years.

I lived on custard. Not a day went by without the yellow nectar, flowing smoothly from bowl to mouth. Sure, I ate other food: potatoes, very little bread, but loads of biscuits. While other kids got football rigs and bikes for Christmas, I got tins of biscuits and sachets of custard. While the family got Christmas pudding I got custard. Not custard and Christmas pudding, just custard.

My Granny was called Granny, a light darkly-clothed figure; neat, with a small wrinkled face and shining eyes set well in, her narrow pointed nose just like mine and her wiry hair always in a bun. On occasions, like early in the morning, I would see her, hair hanging over her shoulders and dressed in her night clothes. She wasn't the Granny I knew, but some younger shadow. I loved my Granny's dinners, traditional fare, but always followed by custard, tea and a special pastry bought that very morning. This was an emporium of custard. It couldn't be bettered.

Years later I went to Granny's home for my lunch, skipping over the cracks and edges of paving stones on the way. Hers was a sloping terraced house five minutes from the school gate. A warm blazing fire in the little backroom provided a welcome. The cat, ever present outside on the window ledge, perched beside a blue ceramic potted plant of ill-determined health. Every day, the same cat and the same plant perched outside of the window. A huge dresser littered with silver plates and bowls occupied one wall. A television and radio sat in the corner above the bookcase. A broken tile in the hearth drew my eye daily. Why was it never fixed? A fat leather sofa filled the remainder of the room, leaving a narrow passage on a threadbare-threatening carpet. An air of decaying wealth and respectability hung in this room. It even hung around my Granny.

A Bump on the Road

My grandfather, Granda, was a shock of thick white hair, appearing at lunchtime, dressed immaculately in waistcoat and bow-tie - a retired chairman of the local council, suffering ill-health caused by the gas in the First World War. He had joined up at sixteen, lying about his age. A horse-riding general was looking for a batman and he volunteered, thinking he would be working with horses. "What's a batman?" he thought. It was too late, when he found out. Later, he was shipped home after suffering dreadful injuries as the result of being gassed. I never talked to him much, not that he was unfriendly, but it just never happened. Occasionally Granda would have a coughing fit, spitting his rejected mucous onto a torn sheet of newspaper before flinging it into the jumping fire. His main interest was horse racing, and he was often found listening to the results on the radio, nipping across to the bookies, or simply chatting to anyone passing his door, where he often stood. He liked custard too. When we were served it, he winked at me across the table. We all liked custard.

Within a cupboard in the dresser lay my money box; Granny gave me pennies for spending and pennies for saving. A shop lined by bottles of boiled sweets, inhabited by two stern sisters, a 1d glass of lemonade was procured. Winter and summer, I had a very happy and nourishing time in that warm and secure world. She impressed upon me that we, our family was a cut above the rest, detached by privet hedge, iron gates and her decaying sense of social position. We were – a people apart. This state of affairs was well known, even the way we pronounced our surname was posh, or so they said.

In the morning I was often left at the school gates by car well before it was fashionable for the middle classes. Mind you, it was at ten minutes past eight on damp and chilly mornings with school not opening until nine o'clock. I stood there, stranded, or perhaps with some other hapless trainee scholars. I was seven or eight years old.

Ten minutes later, up popped the roof-light window in the tiny one-story house opposite. Maggie, hair disarrayed over her night-dress, blaspheming, "Do yous not realise school doesn't open until nine? I have a good mind to send yous home, and stay in me warm bed. Jee-sus

A Bump on the Road

Christ, Honest to Go-ad! Here, young fella, here's the keys." The school keys were tossed from the open window, landing with a clatter in the gutter. I opened up the school on numerous occasions, accompanied with the same scowling, the same spitting and venom. I unlocked the gates and front door and stayed in the foyer until the first teacher came. Or when herself from across the street came into the school - her breakfast on her clothes, on her face and in her mouth. I would then be chased into the playground. Forty minutes later, my sisters, billeted in navy, would wave as they strode uphill to the convent grammar. I impatiently awaited their wave for a drop of the oul' solace. Why wasn't I with them? Too much custard and biscuits, I suppose.

On cold days we went into the boiler house, the chapel, or down to my Granny's or her next door neighbour's. This house was full of life, steam and heat. Girls and boys; half-dressed, bra-chested girls were unseen in my house, but freely observed here. A glimpse into someone else's world - even the tea and toast tasted better here, real life comprising of hot, strong tea and toast and half-naked men and women, a cacophony for my eager senses. Sometimes I got custard. I think they liked to see my reaction when I got it. Normal, fun-loving and generous-hearted people, caring for someone else's child who loved custard.

This was the shroud of security and social position indoctrinated and cast within my genes - laughable in retrospect, but clearly identifiable in the present and proud to have been part of it. These people, aspects of remembered characters and captivating memories, the custard, the childhood pernickety, in essence, my roots, flowing through my veins - the Guinness of my Childhood.

A Bump on the Road

Glorious Morn

It was an hour before midnight on the twenty fourth of December 1966 and 'O Holy Night' was being sung on the radio. It had been planned that every radio station in Ireland, England, Scotland and Wales would play this famous carol at this hour. Also known as 'Minuit, Chrétiens,' tonight would be sixty years after it was first played on radio. Indeed they say it was the first piece of music ever to be played on radio. This Christmas carol event, 'Cantique de Noël,' had been talked about for months in school and in our town and we had all been actively encouraged by the local parish priest to listen on Christmas Eve. Tonight was also my first opportunity to go to midnight mass on my own. My father and mother were otherwise occupied; my father was putting in a new clutch in his car in the garage and my mother was busy preparing for Christmas Day.

Mother was the sole arbitrator of our spiritual life. She guided our prayers at bedtime and held family rosaries in the evening, but really she was more of a cultural Catholic than one with a personal faith, more socially aware of her neighbours' impression.

Of course, Father O'Connor, our parish priest, whose fist, if not ironclad, was perhaps leather-gloved, shepherded us on matters spiritual and pastoral. He was quite an old guy, ambling about the town and church grounds with his walking stick, a shock of white hair and thin eyes and a seemingly ever-expanding waistline. I suppose he didn't wander into the parishioners' houses much these days. He always greeted everyone with a wide smile and in turn received a salute or tip of the hat. His rosy cheeks, purple nose and rotund figure give the appearance of a friendly man. However, while he commanded respect, most people avoided him except when necessary. Except those 'Altar Joes' who perceived that getting to heaven merely required hobnobbing in obedience to a parish priest.

Fr. Donevan was an assistant curate, freshly released from training and full of youthful enthusiasm, wanting desperately to be loved by his parishioners. Mostly, he was mothered by the ladies and patronised by

A Bump on the Road

the men. Though, he was loved by all the youngsters, a breath of fresh air, in his youthful and amiable manner. The religion classes he conducted in the local school were beginning to be something of a legend, known for his fine rendition of 'KumbaYa, My Lord' on the guitar. But this was an uneasy alliance in the Parochial House: between the old and new, the domineering and populist.

Fifteen minutes before midnight I set out into the crisp starlit Christmas Eve with the chorus of 'O Holy Night' ringing in my head. I was full of hope and joy for this was the festival of Christmas, the best time of the year, the night when Christ was born. Everyone's mood was upbeat, exuberant greetings of "Merry Christmas!" shot out of the darkness as a walking train of mass-goers headed up the hill to St. Patrick's. I enjoyed my own company, yet relished the palpable human warmth on this chilly night.

Thoughts of new beginnings, the season's bounty, and of course the special dinner and presents the next day fuelled my Christmas cheer. As my mother would say, hope it snows on Christmas Day because no one has to travel. Snow flakes would certainly be the icing on the cake tonight. Yes indeed, the stars shone brightly on this most holy of nights, the night of the dear saviour's birth.

Here we all are, neighbours, family and friends walking up the hill to the chapel, filled with human weakness and yet through his birth, as the hymn says our fragility is excused. Our souls full of hope, Christmas shopping done, turkeys cooking in the oven, weary travelers home for glorious Christmas morning and Christmas carols sung all over the world. 'Hark, the Herald Angels Sing' heard across the land and many more the children have been practicing in school for weeks.

I approached the church and watched crowds slowly step through the doors on this divine night. I made my way towards the front, wanting to be close to the altar. This night almost everyone fell to their knees to say their prayers as the church filled to the brim. Erring souls saved by his birth, the mood expectant. I hoped Father Donevan would be saying

A Bump on the Road

Mass as he always spirited his way through the service and his sermons were straightforward, short and usually funny.

As I sat up after saying my favourite prayer, St Patrick's Breastplate, 'Christ be with me, Christ beside me…,' followed by a Hail Mary. I shifted over on the seat to make way for Mr. and Mrs. Singh. Mr. Singh was our one and only Indian. Mr. Singh was toffee-coloured, cheerful, smelt of curious spices and hated the British. I guessed all Indians were just like Mr. Singh.

I also knew an Italian family, they were cheerful too - liked to chat, always singing and ran a cafe. They also loved their children more than the Irish because they held the best birthday parties. I had been at two of them, my friend Claudio celebrated his eighth and ninth birthday in their cafe with ice-cream, chips, balloons and games. Each child got a goody-bag filled with sweets when going home.

Mr. Singh was not a Catholic, but his wife was. He met her in Manchester where she worked as a nurse and he worked on the buses. They met on his bus which passed her hospital every day. His cheerful charm worked its magic and as both hated living in England, it was natural they should come to live in his wife's home town. Mr. Singh settled easily and with his natural jovial personality he made a decent living selling carpets door to door. A multicoloured mat lay in front of the fireplace in our front room, testament to his sales skill. Mrs. Singh, Nell, worked in the local hospital and she and her husband lived close to the church in a neat little bungalow. By talking to everyone he had become a local identity, his tan face standing out in a sea of grey pallor. Mr. Singh attended mass with enthusiasm; he seemed to love everything about Irish life, even the weather. He joked that he didn't need the sun as he had a permanent tan. This little joke went down well with locals. He loved the Catholic services, the bells and whistles, the pomp and ceremony, the colour and the drama.

The choir embarked upon the service with 'Oh! Come All Ye Faithful.' The congregation rose, heralding the start of mass. Fr. Donevan entered in his golden chasuble, followed by six altar boys of varying heights and

A Bump on the Road

hair colours. Fr. O'Connor followed slowly, hobbling to a chair with his walking stick, and sat on the left of the altar. I was pleased that the younger priest held centre stage, the main celebrant. He beamed to the overflowing congregation,

"In the Name of Father, the Son, and the Holy Ghost."

He held a short pause before bellowing,

"A Happy and Holy Christmas, this wonderful morning to ye all!"

Immediately the congregation breathed a communal sigh of relief, they were put at ease and everyone glanced at each other, realising they would be home before long and would have their consciences and ears eased as Fr. Donevan would give a light and refreshing, yet spiritually uplifting sermon on this glorious morn.

The choir, positioned in the balcony, sounded its best with the people joining in on the most popular Christmas carols. Hearts were uplifted. A boy soloist in front of the altar began 'O Holy Night', his ice-clear soprano expressing our joy for this night of hope, this night of nights. His piercing voice sent a shudder down many spines and hair stood on many necks. The choir and congregation in unison sang the chorus, 'Fall on your knees! Oh, hear the angel voices.' Well, I can't say angel voices raised the roof of our ancient parish church in the first minutes of the twenty-fifth of December 1966, but a more passionate rendering of this carol I will never hear again.

Beaming from the pulpit, Fr. Donevan nodded to the shepherds, and then lit a candle, an indication for all of us to light our own. The lights in the body of the church were switched off. Mr. Singh, beaming as well, helped light all the candles in the pews around us, embracing this form of communal worship. A candle was lit inside a star at the head of the possession and held high. So, in a candle-lit church in the north west of Ireland, led by a star, the shepherds walked up the central aisle to pay homage to the baby Jesus in the cradle. The little nativity scene at

A Bump on the Road

the side of the altar was strewn with straw. I was worried that a dropped candle could ignite the straw and this moving scene at the crib would run in panic in the direction of the door. But all went well and we prayed to our Lord, thankful we were in this place of fellowship.

Everyone was smiling. Fr. Donevan had no doubt orchestrated these enjoyable activities, and even the old priest was moved by our stooped pious worship. Fr. Donevan then read the gospel: Isaiah 9:2-7. Heartfelt, he paused deeply at many words for their meaning to filter to his congregation. He repeated the extract 'For a child has been born for us, a son given to us; authority rests upon his shoulders; and he is named Wonderful Counselor, Mighty God, Everlasting Father, Prince of Peace,' The choir sang 'Joy to the World,' and tears swept across many cheeks as the carol finished.

The lights were switched on again, and some extinguished their candles as Fr. Donevan, broadly grinning, began his sermon.

"My dear people, on this most holy, of holy night the Prince of Peace was born and we are reminded that Jesus was born in a lowly manger. He was born, just like you and me in a lowly position, a son of a carpenter. He understands our trials, our weaknesses, how sometimes we feel strangers in our own house and even within ourselves. We are strangers in our land, in our own town. We are not masters of our own destiny. The Prince of Peace, Mighty God, the Wonderful Counsellor has a job for us all, if only we look to him for it. If only we bend to his will, not our will. We are not slaves; we are a free loving people, a peaceful people, a free Irish people, chained to the yoke of the British so called empire."

At this point I noticed Fr. O'Connor stir in his seat, his two hands firmly pressed on top of each other on top of his stick, as he shuffled his hips to the edge of his seat. The priest in the pulpit continued.

"My dear people, the chains that bind us are our own weaknesses, our trials that can burden us, and we are bent with its weight. I say to you

A Bump on the Road

bend only to our Saviour, Jesus Christ, unshackle yourself by finding the true light of Christ. Burden him with your worries, ask him to release us from these burdens, release us from the bondage of the British oppressors, we are not slaves, we are a proud and free people. Isaiah tells us – 'For the yoke of their burden, and the bar across their shoulders, the rod of their oppressor, you have broken as on the day of Midian. For all the boots of the tramping warriors and all the garments rolled in blood shall be burned as fuel for the fire'. With the Prince of Peace we will unburden the rod of the oppressor – the British Empire. God is love, born on this most holy of holy nights. Yes, love your neighbour, a Jew and a Catholic wrote that lovely carol, 'O Holy Night'. If they can join together in unity and peace and friendship, so can we. God is peace but how can we find peace with our lands occupied by the British oppressor – the rod of our oppressor."

At this last word Fr. O'Connor was on his feet, shuffling towards Fr. Donevan, unseen.

"My dear people, we are slaves if we let the British chain us. Jesus, the Prince of Peace taught us to love one another, yes, his gospel teaches peace. But how can we find peace when the British occupy our land?"

An almighty crack thundered through the still church. Fr. O'Connor slapped his cane on the edge of the pulpit. Fr. Donevan swung his head round in shock, his face reddening, his eyes widening in horror, as if waiting to be struck by the cane himself. All eyes followed Fr. O'Connor to the centre of the altar as he commenced reciting the Apostle's Creed and slowly the congregation joined with him, hesitating at first but then following his lead. Everything changed; the atmosphere became hurried and tense. Before long, communion was served to the people with the two priests on either side of the altar rails, the choir filling the void and raising the mood of the church once again. The final blessing took place as the elder priest strode off as fast as he could leaving the other priest and altar boys behind.

As the animated congregation left the church we all knew what was on their lips.

A Bump on the Road

I followed Mr. Singh and his wife outside as we dallied home on the cool starry first hour of Christmas Day.

"That was an interesting service, I'll not forget this Midnight mass for a long time," he quipped. "And those hymns were pure sweet joy, the chorus was mighty. The choir did themselves proud. Praising the Lord tonight was a very interesting experience. I can see where the power and the glory are centred in this parish", he said, chuckling to himself.
I asked him, "What are doing for Christmas Day?"

"Oh, nothing much! Probably have a quiet day, hopefully in silence", he smiled. I didn't understand what he was saying. Why would anyone want a quiet Christmas Day?
"You're not a Catholic?"

"Oh, yes, I am a Catholic, and a Christian, and a Muslim, and a Jew and a Buddhist, but mostly a Hindu," he said, bursting out laughing.
 He was one odd guy, I thought, but catching his Christmas jollity I ran off towards home wishing them a Happy Christmas. I was already thinking of breakfast chocolate from my Christmas stocking, turkey and roast spuds for dinner, Christmas charades afterwards but most importantly the presents Santa would bring.

A Bump on the Road

Incident

I was balancing my scrawny bum, rocking on its pointy bits beside the cool kerb, and flicking dust nowhere with a discarded lollypop stick. My father referred to my rear as 'two eggs in a hankie' - when I climbed upon his knee, my two pointy bits dug into his knee, or so he pretended. I found the stick in the gutter, a gully I frequently perused for windswept minutiae or rain-deposited debris. This chilly Saturday, the usual for most summer mornings, grey clouds gently floated amidst the blots of blue casting a smeared light over the street.

A few people wandered about their chaotic chores; our coal man had left a trail of black dust on the pavement, having shouldered the bloated bags on their leather pads to our coal shed, some early birds on the way to town, some to work and one or two neighbours tending to their gardens. The coalman, Mr. Diver, leather-caped, used the side entrance to the back yard, dumping the black stuff in our darkened, dusty shed. The summer was a time to stock pile coal for the rest of the year. In one corner, gritty slack formed a screed slope for overnight banking of the fire. My mother lit the backroom fire on most evenings, not just the centre of winter warmth, but also a means to dry our damp clothes and ourselves.

After the Saturday night's bath, we collected in front of the hearth to watch our favourite TV programmes, seeing our heroes battle once again against evil. It was the family room where we ate, talked, gathered and watched the television during most evenings. Sometimes my mother lit the fire in the good room and knit quietly, leaving the family to watch the television next door.

Although tempting, I refrained flicking the trail of black stuff as I was wearing my clean clothes, and would suffer my mother's fury if I got one mark on them. While waiting for my parents to go shopping and, afterwards, to visit relatives in Donegal, I got out of their way, went outside and flicked the grit in the gutter. I had been waiting all week for this day, a distraction from the long dull summer holidays, a chance to listen to my grandfather's stories and be in his welcoming company.

A Bump on the Road

Opposite, I saw my mate, Tom, up at his parent's bedroom window. They were all just rising. He pulled the curtains and opened the window - he was still wearing his pyjamas. He hoarsely shouted down to me:

"I'll be out after my breakfast."

"I have to go to the shops and visit my Granny in Donegal," I replied shouting up to him.

He turned his head away, as if someone was saying something to him and then, turning back towards me again slightly, raised his hand a bit and was gone as the net curtain fluttered out through the open window.

I looked up on hearing two jeering boys cycling down the small hill in the crescent, their heads and backs parallel to the road, towards me. The first boy wore a brown and yellow-striped tee shirt, brown shorts and plastic sandals. The rider behind was merely a blue flash, but I saw that it was John Crossley and Michael Ramsey, boys from the street. When they spotted me, they veered in my direction and rode their bikes almost on top of me, forcing me to jump onto the pavement to avoid a tangle of bikes and boys. They yelled something like 'Neee Yung,' mimicking racing motorbikes. Within a few seconds they were gone, sweeping up the back lane of the cul-de-sac and disappearing as quickly as they had appeared, leaving a haze of dust.

I gingerly stepped into our garden to avoid the dust shower covering my clothes. The breeze carried it over to the bushes and trees at the bottom of the cul-de-sac, where it settled on the leaves. The little pyramids of dust and grit I built in the gutter destroyed in the scurrying rampage.

After the dust was scattered to the wind, I sat down once again on my kerbside perch, behind our new car, the latest model in lime green poised on shiny black tyres. It was forbidden to play anywhere near my father's proudest possession. There was still no sign of him coming out to perform his Saturday morning routine on the car checking liquid levels in the engine and the window screen reservoir, and looking for any car body smears or scrapes as he walked around the car, kicking each tyre in turn. Eventually, he came out, still newfangled with his toy, unlocked the car, sucked in the pungent ambience of the unspoiled upholstery and started it. He let it idle to warm up the inside, and, looking around the back, he dusted the front facia with his hand. After getting out again, he opened the bonnet to check the levels, walked around the car, and of course, kicked each tyre in turn.

When finished, he stood on the corner of the pavement, his right hand to his chin, eyes aglow, and gave a little smile, more of a smirk, before tossing his greying head to the side and walking with purpose back into the house, for the benefit of any peering neighbours. He always seemed to have something else on his mind as he barely noticed me, sitting nearby. Even if I had called to him, he would have looked in my direction but not really seen me. Our car, as usual, was parked outside the house, in the cul-de-sac, a natural turning spot for cars. I had not seen any cars using it today.

A few locals were walking through the crescent, a sequence of bubbles, although at times they formed a continuous stream. The crescent, a thoroughfare, led directly over the bridge and into the town centre. As the morning wore on, the stream of wives and children made their way there for the Saturday morning shopping ritual. Today was warm enough for wearing a top, like a cardigan, a perfect day for shopping and meeting friends and relatives. Most importantly, it was fine enough to chat in the streets, instead of dashing inside the shops to escape the inclement weather.

Neighbours were beginning to move from their slumber. I could hear the scratch of metal windows forced opened, and through them conversations carried, radios played, toilets flushed, kettles whistled, and the appealing smell of toast, bacon and eggs, potato bread, black and white pudding, the Ulster Fry, buoyant in the suspended dust. Birds flew low, the crows' yarking their presence on rooftops, the sparrows twittering and scolding in the trees, hung on the whispers of the street. The Crescent was awake and at breakfast.

A Bump on the Road

I heard a low roar from the top of the street and looked up. The growling grew as a couple of Saracens sped into view and down towards me. For a second time, I jumped onto the pavement, before they passed me and stopped in the cul-de-sac.

I stood watching a moment and deemed it best to go inside. However, I changed my mind and hooked myself onto the bars of the garden gate. From the relative safety of the garden, I watched the pair of green lumpy armoured vehicles idling outside. The thudding of their engines roared into snarling revs as they juddered in reverse, out of the cul-de-sac. The engine whined on the change of gears, and I saw the driver and his passenger laugh through the post box slits on the vehicle's side. The two six-wheelers turned around and reversed back into the cul-de-sac with their noses facing towards the top of the crescent.

Thankfully, they missed my father's car. The farthest vehicle drove forward and reversed again into the cul-de-sac, swinging left with speed, into the lane and bushes, attempting to position itself in the laneway as fast as it could. It failed. I heard the cheers from inside, as the fresh faced driver tried to manoeuvre the ungainly mammoth around but mounted the footpath and stopped short of a garden wall and another parked car. He reversed further, crushing the wire fence into the hedge as far as he could. The chants from inside reverberated against the hushed breakfast noises of a Saturday morning.

Curtains were twitching as the occupants drawn to their windows by the noise, peered out to locate the source of the thunderous revving. As the driver could not reverse any more, he revved the engine, drowning out all normal sounds of life and nature.

Grinning, as the young soldier revved the engine to move forward, John Crossley rode furiously down the lane, attracted by the noise too, and not expecting to have his way in the lane blocked by the brute. His face whitened, eyes wide and mouth drooping, as he became aware that he was about to crash into a great green lump of military hardware. John did not have a chance to avoid the collision.

54

A Bump on the Road

He rode straight into it; his bike slid underneath as the poor boy splattered into the Saracen. He melted off the side, sliding to the ground like a rag doll, as if in slow motion. The Saracen roared with power and accelerated, its back wheel crushing the bike. Luckily, while the bike went under, John escaped the brutal force of the wheels; the two vehicles drove away up the crescent, its occupants oblivious to the accident. They would not have heard anything.

Michael Ramsey cycled into view and did not see a thing, just John lying on the road. Ashen faced, he dashed to his side, beside the mangled heap of a bike.

As the roar of the Saracen faded up the street, neighbours poured from their homes in various states of dress, all running to John, his crumbled body at the bottom of the lane. Down their paths and onto the street, they shouted, fists gesturing at the grunting carriers.

The soldiers must have heard or seen some of the commotion behind them because the Saracens stopped at the top of the crescent. Their doors stayed closed as they sat inside their vehicles. A man ran up to one and talked through an open slit on its side. Eventually, they disembarked and took up defensive positions behind garden walls and the armoured cars' doors.

 A crowd formed around John, led by a woman in a pink and white dressing gown who bent over him, her fingers moving furiously over the badly bruised and shocked boy. The woman in pink and white was a visiting nurse who pronounced John OK. He tried to get up off the ground and away from the ring of worried faces and eager hands. Michael and I, too, were some of those keen faces peering at his confused eyes, confused at what was before him, his ears ringing with advice not to move. As the nurse testified that no bones were broken, Mr. Watts, a stout man with Popeye-like forearms, cradled John like a newborn babe, and took him to the nearest house.

A Bump on the Road

Noisy guttural sounds and expletives of anger replaced the morning's usual cosy crackling of eggs and bird songs; the crescent was not at breakfast anymore.

Later, with neighbours still in knots of gossip, a gang of youths appeared from the side street, half way up the Crescent, and started pelting the soldiers with anything they could find. 'Fuck Off!' The coarse echo reverberated throughout the street.

Suddenly, two police land rovers, with sirens wailing, swept through the rioters and stopped beside the crowd of adults, outside the house where John lay. The police jumped out of their vehicles into defensive positions as an officer talked to the group of men gathered. Nodding heads turned their attention to the cracks of the small stones bouncing off the Saracens.

A short time later, the ambulance arrived and moved its way through the youths who spread out between the soldiers, the police and the local men. The senior officer, eyes bowed, continued nodding sagely, as if at a funeral, to some of the local men, all, ignoring the stone throwers. Several officers kept a solicitous eye on the streets, protected behind their land rovers. After conferring with the senior officer, some local men marched up to the youths to dissuade them from any further disturbances. Minutes later the youths, dispersed up the side street, shortly reappearing in groups in the cul-de-sac, wanting to watch the craic.

 Once the street was quiet, the senior police officer scurried up the street to the soldiers. Slowly, they withdrew to their vehicles, and drove off, revving their engines in a tantrum. The policeman walked solemnly down the crescent again, all local eyes on him.

Unexpectedly, a crack, more a dull thwack, rang throughout the crescent. Every head turned towards where they thought it had emanated from, the top of the crescent, as everyone dropped to the ground simultaneously, aware of the devilish possibility of the shot. Michael and I had managed to slip in behind the ambulance men and

A Bump on the Road

see John on the sofa covered in a green and yellow bedspread. Mrs. Brown, the owner, spotted us and told us to leave.

We were on our way out the door, just about to step outside, when we heard the single shot. We dropped back inside the hall. The sound of screams brought everyone down to earth, as they lay on the dusty ground. Some, like us, had gone back into their houses, and the police had crept further behind cover. Their eyes and guns in their ready-to-shoot hands scanned the top of the crescent, the source of the firing. Some old hands got up and shouted 'they're gone'; the police fidgeting and nervous, suspicious a bullet could come from anywhere or anyone.

After what seemed like an age, the police climbed into the land rovers, the engines started up and their doors banged shut. The officer still lay in the open road; gun in hand, the obvious target. A land rover sped up to him, a door opened, he climbed in and the two vehicles quickly exited the crescent.

People got off the ground and dusted themselves down, forgetting about young John Crossley and the ambulance crew inside caring for him. We were quickly reminded of John's accident when the ambulance men brought him out on a stretcher, conscious, bruised, and very confused. He could not remember what had happened. The ambulance drove off with one of the local mums, as John's was not about. Some kids went to his house to inform his parents that he was in hospital. The adults stressed to the kids to tell them that he was OK, and was only going to hospital for a check-up.

Once the ambulance had left the crescent, some men and kids went looking for the bullet. I overheard people chatting about the shooting, exclaiming how mad the shooter was, and how lucky the locals and kids were, with so many in the street. Most drifted back to the security of their homes.

I rushed over to my mate Tom, standing at his front door.

A Bump on the Road

"Did you see all that? Wha-OOH, I saw John crash into the Saracen and they didn't even notice it inside!"

"Git in now," a disembodied voice came from within Tom's house.

"Seeya," says Tom as he turned and shut the door.

Now it was all over, the adrenaline was abating and my mates and I were feeling disappointed as all the commotion subsided. My mother was at our door too, and signalled me in.

'Right," says she, "let's have something to eat, banana sandwiches, and then get into the car, and get away from this madness. We'd better be off soon as it is mid afternoon and we intended to leave before lunch." My father came in after me, whispered to my mother, and before long we were in the car ready to go. As we exited the crescent, a queue of cars snaked around the corner, waiting at an army checkpoint. When our turn came for searching, the army officer asked for Dad's licence and told us to get out of the car. We stood on the pavement for more than five minutes as a squad searched the bonnet, boot and inside the car. It took more than half an hour before we were, at last waved through the checkpoint, not having exchanged a single word with the soldiers. My father muttered something like 'talk about the shutting the gate when the horse has bolted' and shortly we were over the bridge and into Donegal. "The shopping can wait," my mother said to no one in particular.

A Bump on the Road

Free Range

Uncle Danny sold eggs. Every Friday my family went to his farm and help him collect, clean and pack the eggs. In exchange for the few hours' work, we could take as many as we wanted. We took dozens, not just for ourselves, but to sell to aunts, friends and other relatives that lived nearby. The journey back home was fraught. The eggs packed in the boot and on our laps turned my mother into a nervous wreck. Never a great passenger at the best of times ferrying the eggs strained her nerves so much that my father declared every Friday night, upon getting home safe and sound with not a cracked egg to be seen, "That's the end of the egg run."

My mother kept a wicker basket on her knee full of shitty free range eggs that she covered with a linen tea towel, such were her sensitivities.

My father called my mum "Mum." except when he was angry with her or us; then he used her Christian name. My Mum called my father "Father."

One evening on the way back over the bridge, aptly named the 'Camel's Hump', the car jolted.

"Father, you're driving too fast! Slow down."

Instead of slowing the car down, Father slowed his words and in a Texan drawl replied,
"Mum, stop fretting. You're gripping the handle of that basket so tight your knuckles are white."

"Father, I am wearing white gloves."

It took a minute before the hilarity of the conversation dawned on us and, as usual, it was my comedian of a brother who burst into laughter first. I don't think my father made his declaration of ending the egg run that particular Friday evening.

A Bump on the Road

During the summer we collected eggs for my Uncle Danny from some farmers because he couldn't keep up with the demand for his eggs. We went to several places. One particular farm was up a deeply-rutted, almost vertical lane.

The farm house was newly built, a 1960s bungalow, a not unlike our own. Except, inside, the absolute basics of living: bare painted walls, bare cement floors, hard chairs, a range burned for heating and cooking, although I always felt cool in their kitchen. A lone sofa sat opposite a cabinet on the other side of the kitchen - that was the sitting room. It had central heating; its radiators were never warm to my knowledge. I used the bathroom once and it too contained the barest necessities. There was no television, but a radio sat on the mantelpiece. A single photograph of the British royal family above the back door was their only ornamentation. Like their home, the farmers were austere and cool. They were a dour couple, characters straight out of the famous painting we had studied in class, *American Gothic*.

Whatever they were feeding them, their chickens produced heaps of crap-covered eggs. No attempt was made to wipe off the remnants of their mucky birthplace. A midden sat pungent near the chicken coops. We would collect a score of a dozen eggs and more.

Father decided one day that he would take the car up the pot-holed lane rather than parking, as normal, at the bottom. He seemed to avoid most of them on the way up. After loading all the eggs into the car, we climbed in to make our decent.

"Holy Mary, Mother of God," my mother erupted, as the car bounced down one pot hole after another - my father twisting and turning the car trying to avoid them, but only ending up in the shuck. The watery drain would not give up its prize – the wheels spun and mud spat in all directions. My brother and I bit our lips, dampening our laughter; it could easily have resulted in a clout from my father's back hander.

"Will we get out and push?"

A Bump on the Road

"Aye."

We lifted the broken eggs and chucked them outside, wiping the seat with Mum's linen tea towel. Luckily, her broken eggs stayed in the basket, or so we thought.

"Dear God, they are soaking through to my skirt!" my mother cried. Father immediately jumped out, opened the boot and retrieved another towel, kept for covering the eggs in the boot. He lifted the basket off my mother's knee and gave it to her. Mum's face was as red as Father's. She couldn't get out as her door was up against the ditch, and I just couldn't see her clamouring over the gear stick and hand brake to get out. We unloaded the eggs from the car and Father sent us up to the farmer to ask him to come down with his tractor to tow us out of the ditch.

It was the first time I had seen the farmer laugh when I told him what had happened. We stood on the back of his tractor seat and down we went to fetch our mortified parents. Within a few moments the rope was hooked onto the car and out it came. Father drove down to the road and my brother and I ferried the unbroken eggs down to the car. It would be a field day or a field night for the rats, rabbits, birds and other wildlife who would feast on the broken array of eggs lying in the middle of the lane. After thanking the farmer, we drove to Uncle Danny's and not a word was said.

My Mum went immediately to the bathroom to clean herself up. After saying hello to my auntie working at her kitchen sink, I went off looking for my grandfather, but he wasn't in the shed nor was he down the ashy path in the garage. I could have spent hours with him, helping out with the garden veggie plot or packing eggs delivered by my uncle in the garage. My brother went searching for my uncle. I had enough of free range eggs.

I ran up the pitted back lane, past the other gardens and garages on my left, and the ditch where we played on my right. At my other auntie's house, the kitchen smelt sweet like a bakery. I looked about downstairs

A Bump on the Road

but found no one. Everywhere was tidy, bloated with ornaments and cushions. I called my aunt's name, but no answer came. In the yard I finally found her. Auntie Thelma was in the shed sewing some curtains in the corner, her sewing corner, as she called it, on a huge industrial sewing machine. She sat under the dingy window, away from the lawn mower, the dog kennel, other bits of stored tools and paints, and boxes of goodness knows what. There, bent over her work, she sewed a strip for the curtain hooks onto some very heavy, wine-coloured floral curtains.

"Ah, hello youngster," she caught my presence with the corner of her eye. "Are you after the boys? They are out in the field, you'll find them there. But first, go into the kitchen, and under the drying cloths on the table, you'll find some fairy cakes. Take two."

"Thanks, a lot!" I yelled as I ran back into the kitchen and took the cakes. Auntie Thelma baked the yummiest cakes in our family. They just melted in my mouth. As I went off down the lane and into the field, climbing through the bars, I held my second bun carefully in my hand.

There was no sign of the boys as I wandered down the well-trodden path alongside the ditch, but I sensed they were watching me. I stopped to finish off the creamy top, the confection making my trip here all the more worthwhile. As I wiped my lips and ensured the crumps went mouth-wards, I scanned the field. The grass was long enough to hide them, but mostly they would be in the ditch, climbing the trees or lying in the water-free shuck.

Phil and Sean, my cousins, were a couple of years younger than me, and "Full of devilment," as my mother would say, "One put the other up to mischief." They were great fun to play with but I would not have dreamt up some things they did. They always seemed to have more fun and more freedom than me - free range cousins. They hid stuff or disappeared for a whole day and reappeared late at night. Threats and thrashings made little difference.

A Bump on the Road

The year before, they had gone into someone's garden and unhooked the glasshouse door from its hinges. Both of them left it hidden in the bushes at the bottom of the garden. No one discovered it for days, but it was the talk of the street. Everybody knew it was them. I acted as their lookout. Thankfully, I was not implicated in this escapade. I knew if I was caught in the act, all hell would break loose, so had worked out my escape plan. My father did not see the funny side of childhood pranks.

When I visited my cousins, they always tried to sneak up on me, pin me to the ground and, if possible, fart on my face. They were great company: always talking, joking, wrestling and giggling. I felt like their third twin. The worst bit would always be trying to keep my clothes clean to avoid a telling off from my mother. Auntie Thelma always told my mother to let me wear my play clothes but, as usual, Mum smiled, turned slightly pink, and let out an imperceptible noise - an embarrassed laugh. She coped with her awkwardness by simply ignoring her sister.

Sure enough, Sean, my cousin accompanied by Peter, another local boy, came out of the ditch roaring and running towards me. I turned to see Phil dropping off the gate and coming towards me from the opposite direction. I was cornered. Phil must have slipped into the laneway on seeing me. I found the best thing was to let them have their fun so I could join them in their latest escapade.

"Charge!" they shouted. I ran into the grass towards Phil, as he was not as rough as his brother, and let him jump me. We tumbled together onto the ground.

Unfortunately, we landed in a cowpat. My clean blue shorts were green with cow-processed grass. We tried to clean it up, but to no avail. Today I was initiated as they had their fun with me, especially with the green, shitty mark on my shorts as my badge of honour.

I knew if I had gone back to my uncle's, I could have gotten something to eat, and more yummy cakes, but I decided to wait until they called me to go home, putting off the lecture about looking after my clean

A Bump on the Road

clothes. I told the boys all about today's incident, and they listened intently. Quick-witted Sean called it an 'eggs-capade' but as soon as the laughter died off they strode off to the ditch to play, as if it was commonplace.

We mainly stayed around the ditch, along the back lane and played, climbing the trees, and then down to skim stones on the river. Little did we know an angler was around the corner and roared at us for frightening the fish. We stayed there until he came towards us shouting some more and chased us from his spot. He had full waders on and ploughed up towards us. I was sure the boys were going to stone him but they left him to his fish.
We walked slowly through the field back to the lane behind the houses, and finally played football against a wall behind my auntie's house.

It was turning twilight on this long cool summer evening when my aunt came up the lane on her way home and told me to go down to my uncle's house, as we were going home. After farewelling them and getting a handful of sweets from a sweetie jar, we were all back in the car for the short distance to home. My father drove very slowly that Friday evening.

It wasn't long before we were having tea and toast and watching an American cop show, the good guy sucking the lolly, wisecracking, as others rounded up the bad guys. The same story line featured every week. When the show was over my brother and I went upstairs to bed.

It was still twilight when I looked outside, the streets deserted, the greying sky setting the sombre mood, blinds and curtains drawn against the night, as the odd wispy streak of smoke disappeared above the chimney. The bathroom was almost chilly when I went to the toilet and finally washed. Getting on my pyjamas and snuggling down under the bedclothes, thinking of nothing as my legs ached with the excitement of the evening and playing with my cousins till late. I had nothing planned for tomorrow, another dull Saturday. The softly creaking stairs as my parents came up was the last thing I remembered.

A Bump on the Road

If Only

Seamas Reynolds played in 'Country Cruisin,' performing mostly country music, Irish style, but this was not Seamas's passion, it was jazz. As he practiced, with the window open, shafts of sun rays bounced off his perfect golden sax, filling the sleepy street with notes of high melodic intensity and sweeping harmonies. He held it between his thick arms, but the sublime sound caused by his unnaturally large throbbing cheeks could stand the hair on the back of the necks of passing locals.

Seamas Reynolds was a legend in the Irish music scene. He was known for being instrumental in starting the whole show band era. When he played, or practiced, he was not just Seamas Reynolds, he was not just the sax, not just the music. This permutation became an emotion - rapture. He disappeared into the instrument and music and the fusion somehow transmuted into the eye of god. They said that when he played, he was a man possessed. His wife was a musician too and his kids grew up in a musical household. If only he had gone to England, they said, he would be rich and famous by now. Elvis heard him on a track recorded for Cliff Richard and wanted him to come to America. But England was the extent of Seamas Reynold's travelling. He went there for a few days at a time and returned home to his wife, kids and pigeons. Pigeons were his hobby, he'd sell them to other pigeon fanciers now and then, but mostly he would just talk pigeons to his mates, escaping from his esoteric music and family life.

A few recordings took him to Dublin or to England, providing good money for holidays and for running a decent, dependable car. He disliked the travelling. The long boring distances were a waste of time, he considered, and afterwards the drunken late nights with colleagues or punters peeved him. He knew the reason many came to the dances - not for his music. He enjoyed watching the floor and the youngsters' shy awkward movements performing the mating dance. But above all, although he enjoyed playing those smoke filled dance halls and pubs, he liked to play his sax. He made a decent living for his family so he was a happy man. Seamas lifted the quality of any performance and provided the country-wide reputation that brought in the crowds for the Country

A Bump on the Road

Cruisin' show band. Most nights, after a beer with the lads, he went home - a dependable home-bird like his pigeons.

His wife, Kay, a talented pianist, with classical tastes in playing and listening that echoed through the house daily. Their children played music too. Rory, the eldest son, was a saxophone player, matching his father's talent. A narrow strap of seventeen, he sometimes played with his father when the need arose, a group put together for special functions. Rory could have played every weekend but his father was careful not to encourage him too much and distract him away from his studies. He had his own band, with a few school mates that played to a younger audience. Like his father, he could pick up an instrument and begin playing a new tune very quickly. His handsome features, mostly taken from his mother, and his musical talent drew the girls.

Seamas grew up in an era of poverty, with little opportunity. He was a self-trained musician, and with his wife's encouragement began to play full time. He could have worked seven days a week; there were dances every night in every county. Parish priests realised the weekly dance in their parochial halls was a great money earner. Friday or Saturday night, people got dressed up, posed for the opposite sex, some got lucky and danced away the worries of a dull existence.

Seamas went to England to record with some of the more famous singers or Irish groups: Cliff Richard, Val Doonican, The Clancy Brothers and The Bachelors.

However, one lasting impression of England left Seamas quite certain the country wasn't for him. He was staying in a bed and breakfast with other English musicians when he was recording for Cliff Richard and noticed a sign while having his breakfast. It was turned back to front and Seamas knocked it by accident. It read – 'No Irish or Blacks'. He showed it to his companion who just smiled and said, "It's amazing what a famous name like Cliff Richard can do! Gets an Irishman a bed for the night." Seamas retorted that he played black music anyway so was in good company.

A Bump on the Road

The Reynolds saw the benefits of education, to provide a better start in life for his kids. Rory was their hope - to study at university, maybe a doctor or something professional. His musical talents outshone his academic though, so a music degree would do him just fine. Their other children would have the chance to study at university too. Seamas let his wife do the cajoling and encouraging them in their homework and examinations.

Rory was becoming a talented performer and showed a lot of promise. He was nearly eighteen and doing his final examinations at the end of the year.

A contrary sort, or, as his mother said to him often, 'a wee thran youngster.' Maybe, 'determined' might be a better description of his trying spirit. Once he got an idea into his head, it stuck. If he got a notion for a certain female, he persisted until he got a date, and that was that. Once he conquered that notion, he moved to his next, but he had many notions and hence many dates with many girls. His father thought it was a good idea and, to a degree, his mother too, but she thought he was bit fickle and wasn't sure his attitude to the opposite sex was totally honourable. It was just another worry that she bore for her children.

Paula, a teenage pop singer, was coming over from England on a short tour. She had a meteoric success with her hit 'Scream' in the British and Irish charts, success which had, unfortunately, caused the breakup of her band. The Irish gigs had been set up months before, and so, rather than break the commitment, Paula's management had decided to do the gigs with a local band. All venues were sold out.

Paula needed a support act that could be the backing group too and Seamas's connection with Cliff got Country Cruisin' the gig. Rory was employed as a sax player for a bigger, fuller sound and when his father played the trumpet. With only four dates, and good money to be made, the Reynolds looked forward to the tour. They rehearsed all the songs that Paula would perform, only the day before their first performance in Belfast.

A Bump on the Road

Seamas noticed immediately that Paula and his son were hitting it off. There was, after all, only a year of difference in age, and his son had enough experience to charm the birds off the trees, even the famous ones. They spent as much time together as possible, childishly giggling their way through rehearsals or deep in conversation before performances. He caught their eyes meeting on many occasions.

The shows went well and in Dublin the musical and media royalty attended. Afterwards, over a few drinks, Seamas was offered positions in some of the most famous show bands, as was his son. Again, Paula and his son spent the evening together. After the encores, the management had arranged a small farewell party in a nearby hotel. Some of the group were staying overnight but the Reynolds drove back home. After fond farewells, Seamas watched his son and Paula embrace and he tried to detect any deeper attachments.

Arriving home in the dawn twilight, the two had some welcome tea and toast and were joined by Kay for five minutes. The next day, Seamas got up at lunch time, planning in his head what to do with his extra earnings. While his son stayed in bed, he left the house to see one of his pigeon fancier friends. It was a bright, showery day, and the sun weakly shone into the kitchen.

Upon returning home a few hours later, something made him stay with his pigeons longer than necessary. He entered the kitchen sensing the sadness and saw Kay, standing stiff, looking out the window. Seamas simply said 'OK?' and she burst into tears, clutching his chest. Rory had left to follow Paula to her home town of Liverpool. His father was angry, but not surprised. 'What about school?' Seamas kept shouting, but he knew his son would not have wanted an argument, so left home before his father came back. That is exactly what Rory would have got; an argument and Seamas would have forbidden him.

The next few days were fraught. Gentle words were spoken and the absence of music was noticeable in the house. The children missed their big brother too. Often, when he came into the house he would chase them, tickling them, and they ran, looking for sanctuary, always moaning about him. Now they wished he would walk in and tickle them forever. No one had imagined this would happen.

At last, one of the local kids came running into the kitchen without a knock, exclaiming 'Rory is on the phone!' The red phone box stood on the corner of the street, where Kay hurried to talk to her son.

The conversation was brief, but Kay was able to work out that Paula and Rory were not romantically involved, or if they had been, it was now over. While happy that he was well, she heard sadness in his voice. Did he regret his big decision? Would his pride be hurt if he returned home? Anyway, Paula was heading off to London to record her latest but she had helped him get digs and found him a spot in a local band.

Weeks went by and life in the Reynolds' family was not easing. They missed the boy terribly but they sensed it was just a matter of time. Rory was playing several nights a week, making some money, and had some female company. He had one tense conversation with his father who had decided to travel to Liverpool in a week or so to encourage him back but Kay knew he would return sooner rather then later.

Rory started to really enjoy playing with a Liverpudlian band, a talented group of young men, who were only starting out themselves, some still at art college. He should have been having the time of his life, and yet he was lonely, despite occasional female company, and unhappy at times without knowing why. Something was gnawing in his gut and a shadow seemed to stilt his thinking.

One night, he was playing with his band in a pub in the docks. Every gig had a few fans and plenty of groupies too. They played mostly rock and roll, well-crafted, the music and lyrics written by members of the group. That night he sat during the break looking out over the docks, and spotted a boat. It was the Belfast overnighter, and it was to depart at eleven that night. It suddenly dawned on him that his unhappiness was homesickness. He immediately told the lads and rushed to the port to buy a ticket. He had time to come back and play for another hour, and John, one of the band members, promised to sort out his stuff from the

A Bump on the Road

digs and send it on to him. So he left the pub with his guitar and a smile on his face, got onto the ship and slept the best sleep he had for weeks. From Belfast, he got the bus to his home town and arrived at lunchtime, receiving hugs and smiles and lots of kisses from his mother and his siblings.

"What did you call the band you played in?"

"Oh, just a new wee band, they were good though. I think they are going to stick with the name - The Beatles."

A Bump on the Road

In for the Day

I was like a child head lifted high
And the bells told the time at 6 o'clock
And I stood still in the sacrament of sound
©www.eamonfriel.com

"If anybody can make ye smarter, it'll be the Christian Brothers. They have a grand reputation for getting ye an education and a decent job. Yip, them brothers'll get ye smarter! Mind you, some say they beat it into ye, I wouldn't know. Master Friel beat it into me, and he had eight childer of his own. I left him as soon as possible, twelve years of age. That was enough for me." His laugh wheezed into a cackle that became a phlegm explosion onto the path, before pulling out his dirty white hanky. Everyone stared at the birds, who, with a flourish of their wings, were building their nests on the bus shelter's eaves. This was the perceived wisdom of an old guy sitting beside us in a charcoal-striped suit, polished at the knees and elbows. His Donegal tweed tie was like my father's, his white shirt worn and thready at the collar - all of us waiting for the bus to the city.

Winter was over: it was a fine spring day. The birds were singing as they built their nests and we were going in for the day, to the big smoke, just the day for a trip to the city, my mother kept repeating. The old man muttered to himself, no one paying him any particular attention, "There's not any trouble here, the film crews are away to the city. There's more stuff going on there. What we need is one big drawer and we'll put them and the past away and turn the key. That would soon sort it out." The passengers were so busy watching the nesting birds that they almost failed to notice that the bus had pulled in. For the length of our journey through small villages to the big smoke we were accompanied by our elderly friend singing to amuse himself and us. The patchwork of green fell away towards the river and the mountains beyond to Donegal, warmed in the hazy sunshine and giving rise to a jolly atmosphere on the bus, like a holiday bus run. I said to my mother, "Look at that sky, it's a beautiful morning" and the snatches of appropriate lyrics rose from the resident singer, 'now a song can make

A Bump on the Road

you sad, but a blackbird can make you glad,' 'music on the breeze, music of delight,' so true. An odd smile from some of the passengers kept him going. The bus stopped here and there as a variety of people got on, all heading to the big smoke for business or pleasure. We would be partaking of both: I was being enrolled into a new school, as my gurgling stomach attested, but afterward we would be tourists, in for the day, doing a bit of sightseeing and shopping.

After getting off the bus we headed straight into the station's cafe. Foggy steam escaped as we opened the door; the room inside was hazy and its windows clouded-up. Billows of steam heaved out of the hot water cauldrons for the copious cups of tea fortifying the transient crowd. Shortly after we sat down to have our break, the smell of musty coats caught in my throat, so I leaned forward to smell the chocolate-coated wafer I had been bought, in its thin silvery-mossy wrapping. My mother had tea and a cream finger and I had a glass of milk with my biscuit. "I needed that," my mother whispered, "to calm me nerves." "God," I thought. "Both of us are nervous wrecks." My stomach churned, apprehensive about going to a new school, and yet excited to have a day in the city.

We went up the hill and through the church grounds for a shortcut. Meeting the principal to enroll me into his big school caused further trepidation; otherwise it was a day in the heart of the town, only in for the day. "Time and again," my mother chuckled, "we travelled to this city, your father and me, just before we got married. Ah, the dreams we had then! It's enough to have dreams and have laughed, your father said, on our way to build our little kingdom of love."

Then she added, "After the school business we'll have lunch in the fancy department store and watch the quality sporting the latest styles." In the afternoon we'd catch the sights and sounds, the bright lights of the shops and do some shopping. She was as excited and as nervous as me.

When we reached the school, its bell rang out. Some church bells tolled their answer: they were having a conversation in the sky, a salutation of

A Bump on the Road

sound, a forbidding welcome. I lifted my head to look at the Brother approaching us, chalk and dandruff on his soutane. The children milling around seemed unaware of us, for all their talk, hunched up in the wind, some dancing on their way to class. We were shown to the principal's office at the final ringing of the bell. He stood in the doorway, shook my mother's hand and beckoned her in. There we parted. "Take a look around you, and as you make your way, see the others try their best." I was to go on a short tour with Joe, a big lump of a pupil.

"Hey, Big Chief, who's that?" some spotty boy asked Joe.

"A new boy."

Joe, 'Big Chief' took me to a classroom. "This is Mr. Joyce, he teaches History, you know, Roman stuff, all about the Kings and Queens of Rome." After seeing the classrooms, the handball alley, Our Lady's grotto and the woodwork and metalwork rooms, we returned to the principal's office. I had a last look down some corridors and wished I was going with Big Chief. "I hope you sing", said the Brother, his bright laughter ringing through the corridor. "You'll have a great time here," he added, speaking those lying lines so convincingly. I knew because they had fooled me before, at my previous school.
After enrolling to become smarter, we went to the city park to see the spring displays. My mother was a keen gardener and nothing gave her more pleasure than working the clay or clipping the climber. The park was on one of the city's many hills. She bent double looking at the name tags of each and every flower and shrub; the red and purple trumpets, the yellow bands of blossoms dancing on the ditch, swaying, swinging, waltzing - the dance of the years. I stood entranced as they whirled in the spring wind.

Spotting a pond, I scouted around and was lucky to find some skimming stones under a struggle of withering wild flowers. I counted their leaps, three, four, five, as the ripples ringed each single stone. I watched the wind across the water causing little waves and causing my skimming stones to bump and dive. My mother called to me just as I was getting into the rhythm. I searched for a final stone: the flattest and

A Bump on the Road

smoothest to spin in the weak sun, the sweetest stone for last. One, two three, four and it dives into the eddy; my final stone, in its flight of fantasy. "Listen," says she, as we stood in the city park, in for the day. "No silence."

Off we went to the post office. Hung next to it was the biggest copper teapot I had seen in my whole life. Underneath, a man played his guitar. I watched him strum, sing of faith and the kingdom to come. Another beaming, smooth-faced man handed me a small leaflet, with a picture of heaven sitting above radiating sun beams. It read: 'Are you ready for the Kingdom of Love? Love is not narrow, for love is a generous thing'. I wondered when my Dad sweet-talked my Mum; did he steal his line from this leaflet?

We had lunch in the swanky department store, watching the quality pass by. "Tell me love, what will we do with all this day, all this bright blue day that stretches far away?" my mother asked. Shopping and more shopping in the bright lights, the throngs pushing and shoving, up and down the hills, my mother's running commentary about one place or another, "there is a river in the hill that turned the wheels of waterwheels. The mills are gone, the wheels are done." I was ready to go home, fed up waiting, carrying the bags, my wheels were done. I wanted to go home.

We went down a side street and walked onto the scene of a street fight; two groups of young men were roaring and fighting, mostly roaring. People were giving them a wide berth and we did too. My mother muttering, "those lovers of hate and haters of love, they have hard hearts, and on this bright sunlit day too!" Mum was ready for home too.

We boarded the bus: many had already taken their seats. My mother and I negotiated our bags down the centre to find a spot. I, of course, got the window seat. Our bags stowed safely above, I heard my mother sigh deeply and relax into her seat. Something disturbed my hair; I looked up to see a hand disappear over the seat behind. I got up and knelt over the back of it, it was the hatted gent with the Donegal tweed tie, only now it had a yellow yolk stain. He asked me if I was going to get smarter with the Christian Brothers. I said I was. He leaned forward and beckoned me to come closer. I leaned towards him and smelt his stale, fag-end

A Bump on the Road

breath. "Did you..., did you...," he stammered. I could see he was forming his words carefully, and speaking slowly. "Did you know you are psychophysiologically unique?"

A Bump on the Road

My Dear Boy

Sorry for not writing sooner, how many years is it now? Your mother and I are well, having moved down-under but we know you're not too far away. Your younger sister and brother have settled well in our new life. He's not unlike you, I imagine, bubbly and enthusiastic about school and everything he does. They are mad about sport here and his teacher has him supporting a footy team already. They are everything we could have wished.

You know this all started in a telephone box. No, that's not strictly true. We had a bit of fun trying to remember where it all began. Was it a sweaty sleepy fumble in the middle of the night or one of those slow sweet-smelling nights of seduction and warmth? I suppose these are things we generally do not talk about to our offspring, suffice to say your mother says you were conceived in Uncle John's in Manchester. Curiously, your mother believes this was where your wee brother was conceived too. As I was only the messenger I will take her word for it. Anyway back to the phone box: traditional red, a Post Office one, not found much today. I think it even had one of those huge, black handsets. We met at lunchtime, as was common practice for us. We have been quite lucky in that respect: wherever or whatever part of the world or country we were lunchtime munchers.

Anyway, this phone box was right beside a village bank, a small substantial single-story building of grey granite; the sort of bank that you see in advertisements - friendly and efficient staff with solid mahogany wood panelling and desks. The bank that likes to say "Yes!" Externally, the window boxes full of sensible blues and reds opposite a triangle of more colourful banks of flowers and a seat for weary customers. Do you like "the colourful banks of flowers?" Is your old man clever or what?

Unfortunately, this picture of rural bliss was somewhat misplaced. Inside the phone box the stench of beer and urine overwhelmed our senses that your Mum's stomach nearly turned. So we stepped outside again for air, this time I held the door open and looked around for

A Bump on the Road

another phone box. The triangle was the convergence of three streets. Add a fourth and you have the centre of this prosperous country town. Well-heeled wives and farming folk milling around were going about their daily business on that unusually warm and sunny February. We could not see another phone box so we decided to persevere and with me standing outside with the door wide open, your mother held her nose to phone the doctor. My joke about her sample not being too different from the perfume of the telephone box was repaid with a dig in the ribs. I further got on her offside by donating an Irish florin that shot through the coin box and cut off the doctor in mid flow. I was sure the doctor must have thought your Mum had a bad cold with her finger holding her nose and was surprised she did not invite her to the surgery for vitamins or something. With correct money in hand she rang back, fraught with anxiety and impatience. The test proved positive.

At that stage you were six weeks old. We considered ourselves lucky, we had found each other, we did not try too long and, you know the joke, it was great fun trying. Overjoyed, was an apt description of our emotions. We were to be modern parents, and improve on our parents' ways with the latest textbooks and theories. It was later we found your Grandparents had much to offer and did exceptionally well raising seven children each, given their circumstances.

Your Mum was not finished in that beer and urine gin palace. This time with joy in her voice and her sense of smell obliterated, she telephoned your grannies and all our friends.

Your impending birth and your development of nine months within did not change our lifestyle too much. My sister gave me a tome called *Pregnancy*, the bible for birth and babies. I remember it was thick and white. The details and advice for preconception, conception, the nine months of your growth, the birth and the first year were all treated with the utmost scientific rigour. It was direct and informative. We charted your daily and weekly development.

Bedtime was about twelve o'clock, fairly normal for our part of the world, although staying up during the wee hours of the morning in

A Bump on the Road

Ireland is not unusual. I usually listened to a music show on the radio. It stopped broadcasting at two in the morning. Admittedly I was well asleep by then. As a concession to your maturity your Mum started to go to bed early and so I went with her and read. This habit has not changed much. Your Granny did this too. Maybe it is old age but we don't seem to get enough sleep these days. The thought of being able to stay awake to two in the morning fills me with youthful jealously.

"Play classical music," the book said. We did. Soon the round swollen belly rose and fell. A bit like my own at the moment! We could feel the hard lumps - feet they said. When the scan showed your head and limbs it became even more real. I used to lie with my head on you, listening, feeling your gentle movements, and sing one or two of the first lines of songs for which I am renowned. Beyond that I falter and pain the listeners. People come up to me in public places such as the supermarket and say things like "Someone's happy." If they had to listen to that one refrain all the time I think I would see the blunt end of their can of beans. I now apologise for those mini concerts although the nursery rhythms weren't too bad, were they?

As you grew your feet and hands became very obvious and we held them and rubbed them, you know. We saw your shoulder turn, or was it your bum? We christened you 'The Bump'. Not very original or charming! You were our bump, our living, thriving, genetically one of us, one of the family. We cherished that time with The Bump and those limb movements. You were carefully bathed and foamed by your mother, looked after just like any baby - a real baby.

You should have seen your Mum making summer dresses on the floor with you; she couldn't easily bend or be very flexible, so I had to help to lay out the pattern. I will not make any suggestions about waddling penguins or beached whales, but your time to join us in the real world was fast approaching. Your Mum had a good pregnancy with you, just a little morning sickness and the dry biscuits and a glass of water by the bedside were not uncommon. More scans, more pre-natal visits, all well.

A Bump on the Road

You were booked into the hospital the night before, no eating for your Mum after six o'clock. They checked you, all was well. You were full-term, indeed a little over. I stayed in my brother's that night as it was closer to the hospital. Tomorrow The Bump arrives and gets a proper name. We didn't have one chosen then.

The phone rang at 5.45am. Could I come into the hospital now? I dressed quickly and drove the short distance on the quiet roads. Still happy and content, I was taken to the scan room. Your Mum was there. She was quiet and looked tired. There was little space so I held her hand. Three or four nurses were there. The nursing sister stood to my right. She said they just wanted to do a scan. She showed us the outline of your body, head and limbs on the small black and white screen. Then she pointed out an area which she said was your heart. She said we should see a little pulse. There wasn't.

The nursing sister was a solid girl, with thick arms. I felt them as my legs folded towards the floor but I think she lifted and pushed me onto your Mum's bed. I couldn't get to your Mum with the equipment and nurses and just held her hand, tighter, tighter. Of course, all were in tears in that room. Your Mum and I were in shock. I eventually held your Mum's head as we wept. I understood now the meaning of a stone in my stomach. The nurse asked about phoning relatives. They needed the scan room and your Mum should give birth to you naturally. How can you give birth to a dead baby naturally? They would make your Mum comfortable and I needed air.

Shouting and roaring, as I drove the car home. What other drivers made of it I'll never know. With radio blasting, engine revving I let it all out. I still use this method. I realised nearly four hours had passed. I phoned your Grandparents and a distressing task it was. Shock waves went through our family circle and friends. Work places became very sombre, I was told. Prayers were said in various churches. We were consoled by everyone's response.

I returned to the hospital, your mum was in an operating theatre with a drip to encourage the birth, it was a stark and clinical place to be. We

A Bump on the Road

embraced and said little. Your Mum's bravery in crisis is legendary. With much respect and deep honour I got to know a lady who drew on hidden depths of courage. How she managed to maintain a sense of proportion and humour, I'll never know. She was more concerned about my sanity and well-being than her own and just imagine what she had gone through and about to go through. We were very ignorant about stillbirths and so were the hospital authorities. We did the best we knew. Your Mum decided, with the nurses and doctor's advice, it was the best to deliver you, but not see you. I left your Mum that night in a storeroom. They said that was the only place available and close to the nursing staff. Both of us exhausted.

When I came back a few hours later you were born. Family crowded around and supported as best they could. We were asked if we wanted to see you. I said I would but we thought at the time, it best for your Mum not to. Today it is very different, babies like yourself would have spent a day with your parents, dressed and chatted to and mourned.

I was taken to a storeroom where you lay on a trolley covered in a white sheet. The nursing sister, the one with the big arms was gentleness itself and lifted the sheet. You were tiny, your body wrapped in a blanket to your neck. You had a little squashed face. Eyes closed, just asleep, a little bruising at the side of your forehead, blackened lips, a baby button nose and blotchy strawberry marks on your cheeks. You unmistakably favoured your Mum's side of the family. I tried hard to photograph your face into my memory. I think I rubbed my finger on your cheek, I am not sure. The most striking feature and memory was the fine covering of reddish hair. I can claim that on my side of the family too. She did ask if I wanted to hold you but I didn't and of course we should have been together as a family. Hindsight is a great teacher.

I saw you again in your little white coffin. We took you to our home town, for burial, in the back of your uncle's Volkswagen Beetle. We were thankful and mindful because the hospital asked if they would take care of you. I had heard later that in previous years you may have been incinerated or buried in an unmarked grave. Now, you are in a grave with your great, great grandparents and if you walk on down the hill

A Bump on the Road

directly from your grave you would find the house where your Mum was born. Your tenth anniversary was celebrated with prayers at your graveside and this was for your Mum as she couldn't make it, the first time.

Even though your grave is miles away now, I know, really know you are near.

A Bump on the Road

Big Pol

Business Studies with Big Pol was always a comfortable option, always the first classroom to empty at lunchtime, always a lengthy discussion of last night's televised soccer match at the beginning of his class. Big Pol got his name, predictably, because of his towering height and his propensity for polo mints. His height helped curtail any class indiscipline. Big Pol's teaching strategy flowed from the horizontal position, his bum on the seat and legs on the corner of the table, the polo mints positioned in front of him. After his opening remarks about last night's soccer, triggering an intense discussion, he allowed open debate of any topic depending upon his mood: history, literature, current affairs. Often he would simply say, "Ask me any question, boys, anything you like". Reading the next twenty or so pages of the textbook followed the discussion. If you had read it, you read more pages or simply dozed in a reading position, in silence. While this worldly contemplation took place, Big Pol read his thriller, the latest, or fed his passion for Raymond Chandler.

The active part of his teaching strategy occurred in the latter part of the lesson a question and answer session. To avoid him asking a question of us, we fired the questions at him. Often, he referred to the book or a diagram for discussion, or he got us to copy relevant definitions and diagrams from chapters. This was his paradigm in every class. The boys liked the easy predictability of this routine, and we always encouraged the interested soccer players in the class to shoot a question at him as soon as he entered the room, hoping someone would ask another before his attention went to the textbook.

While absorbed in a world of espionage or Marlowe, Big Pol let his fingers do the walking: he was notorious throughout the school for his proclivity to work his finger up his nose or up his bum. This he did without any awareness of anyone present. He was a bit of a dandy, a gentleman about town, wore smart shirts, well-cut trousers and highly adorned leather shoes and boots. Buckles dressed his shoes in silver or brass, leather piled on leather with carved intricate patterns. 'A buckle is a great addition to any shoe' - an apt Irish proverb I had discovered in a

A Bump on the Road

short story during the English lesson the previous week. His well-shod feet matched his bejeweled fingers. Silver, gold, and stone rings enfolded them. Celtic filigree produced in silver over emerald worn on his lanky-aged fingers, etched silver bands on his little ones. Different rings appeared frequently. His tight silvery beard covered his thin face; his mouth, almost lipless, and tobacco stained teeth were dominated by his sharp protruding nose, famous for enjoying frequent excavation. Only on close inspection did the surprising discovery of his deep set, beady eyes, betray those determined pupils. While his preponderance for saggy cardigans transposed him from a dapper dresser, a man about town, into a work-a-day teacher, his simmering eyes betrayed a man with a hidden passion.

After five minutes, Big Pol signaled to me to come up to his desk and asked if I could go to the nearby shop to get him some fresh baps for his lunch. I was not the usual errand boy as he always chose a local lad, John Deeney. John was tall, looked more mature for his age, and always encased in a duffle coat. He lived in the same street as the shop. We envied John because he could get out of bed ten minutes before school started and still be on time. In fact, on a few occasions he showed us his pajamas under his clothes. The previous week Big Pol and some of us had been chatting in the playground, idling away our time until recall for class. I summoned up the courage and asked him if I could perform the baps-buying role sometime. He said he would think about it. Therefore, when he called me up to the front, I didn't think it was for buying baps, but something to do with school. I was a quiet, small student, flying below everyone's radar.

"Get me a bap and a cream finger from the shop across the green, can you manage that and not get lost?" He asked me in a squeaky soft sarcastic voice, as he handed me a pound note. "Don't lose me change!" he added, as I made my way to the door.

Outside the door the corridor was empty and I relaxed. Darting down the three flights of duplicate stairs, and glancing up and down the bottom corridor, I hoped for a quiet exit. I particularly didn't want to meet the principal, Brother Browne, whose brisk step of size ten sent a

A Bump on the Road

trail of chalk dust and dandruff in his wake. The foyer was clear, but on approaching the front door I heard a door open and the flap of a soutane. I stepped nimbly inside the medical room, an occasional sixth form study room. It was empty, just a couple of books littered the tables. His steps came towards the room and the door opened a little as I stood behind it, holding my breath, panic flowing through me. Brother Browne must have heard something, but the door closed again quietly. Relaxing, I heard his steps continue down the hall and disappear into silence. Stepping out, the coast was clear again and off I went, through the front door, through the school gate and up to the shop.

I crossed the soggy green, opposite a square of houses, where the corner shop stacked its vegetables outside on pale wooden boxes. Having got my purchases from a craggy faced man in an off-white, stained shop coat that barely looked at me during the transaction; I carefully counted the change and placed it in my empty left trouser pocket. I was determined not to be embarrassed in front of the class or Big Pol as I would have been if the change was incorrect or mixed up with my money or the assorted contents of my pockets. The thought of emptying my pockets in front of everyone terrified me. Keeping the bap and cream finger in good condition was essential, I held the white paper bag containing Big Pol's lunch very carefully. The cream finger positioned on top of the bap, its white greasy filling soaking through the paper already.

I waited on the path to let a bus pass and cross the green again, when alongside me stood a familiar body, curiously wrapped in a large duffle coat. From within its huge hood came a grunting salutation. I did not reply. Was that John Deeney's voice? Was John Deeney in class today? The person hid his hands in his pockets. However, something about the flop of the elbows did not look right. He scurried away across the green, towards the school. I looked at the sleeves of the coat, straining my eyes to see the sleeves tucked into his pockets. His arms were not inside the sleeves. Underneath the long coat, was a thin rifle barrel, just above his ankle, positioned tightly to one side of the trouser leg. This was the purpose of the oversized duffle coat. Slowing down my pace to let him get further away from me, he waddled into a lane next to the school. By the time I got to the gates, he had disappeared.

"What kept you?" A question bawled at every boy tasked to get the baps, and the same answer always came, "there was a queue in the shop". The ritual was completed with me getting a polo mint for my trouble. Leaving class for a short period was a better reward, although seeing a gunman had been unnerving.

I went back to my desk, looking out at the magnificent views down over the town, the cobalt winding river reflecting the clouded-spotted day. The sight of the town nestled on the curve of the river was always welcome relief from humdrum teaching. Through the windows on my left a couple of open fields lay beyond our playing fields, each bounded by tightly grown hawthorn hedges. I could see a group of men gathering under the hedge alongside the school's grounds. It was not unusual to see groups using the field for target practice. The penny dropped - that duffel coat was moving weapons for this target practice session.

Big Pol asked us to continue reading our little red books, and ignore the dozen men milling around the field below. It was difficult. Mostly they stayed close to the hedge and out of sight, while a couple of them placed targets in the centre of the field – one was a round target and the other a dummy. This unreal movie, through the dirt-smeared windows, captured our full attention. We could not see the precise movements of the men but knew full well what was happening. Only the staccato blasts echoing through the sunny morning indicated something was amiss. After what seemed quite some time, Big Pol drew us back to his discussion of how business, in the real world, could make a profit.

Suddenly, all heads turned to look through the windows to determine the source of a great rumbling outside. It was the whoop-whoop of a helicopter's blades, flying across the school's windows. After hovering over the fields, it rose swiftly, realizing what was occurring below. The helicopter dipped again, flew at speed over the field and headed towards us, leaving the windows vibrating in its aftermath.

A Bump on the Road

Big Pol sighed deeply. "Ah! Where were we? Write your questions and we'll start."

Five minutes later, the thundering whirring of three Wessex helicopters came into focus. They hovered over the fields next to the school until, one by one, they disappeared beyond the hedges and rose sharply again. British soldiers dropped into the higher field. We could see clearly their green garb moving along the upper hedges. The Irish Republican Army (IRA) or as they were known locally, the 'Boys' collected in a bunch by the lower hedge. A stream of shots rang out. A sniper had climbed a tree and let off a volley towards the newly arrived troops, who returned fire, scattering the top leaves of the trees where the Boys positioned themselves. Two fields and a hedge separated the warring parties. We had a grandstand view of the battle below, all of us now standing and watching through the windows. Further rattles erupted beneath us, as the British attempted to move forward but the gunmen held their defensive positions. From above, we could advise both parties how to advance given our strategic view.

"Jeeze, boys I guess we better make a move, leave your books", said Big Pol. Just then, a ginger-headed and bearded new teacher stuck his head into the room, shouting, "We will evacuate to the Quad, NOW!" The evacuation bell rang too, and hundreds of boys filled the corridors and stairs leading down to the Quad, a sanctuary from the gun battle above, and below the surface of the main part of the school. The Quad housed the metalwork room on one side and the woodwork room on the other. A pond had been sculptured by the metalwork teacher, and the woodwork teacher planted a garden of vegetables and other various plants. As the boys streamed into the safety of the Quad, they trounced everything in sight, the garden pounded by hundreds of tiny feet. The metalwork teacher stood astride his pond, attempting to save the newly installed fish by pushing away any errant boy. Escape was through a side gate, into a square of houses and down a winding hill.

Arriving in the square we found people going about their daily business, unaware of the life and death battle five minutes away. As we walked

A Bump on the Road

off, we realised our time was our own for the rest of the day. I went to a mate's house for lunch on the other side of town to plan what to do with our unexpected freedom.

A Bump on the Road

The Deliverance of Destiny

The sand stung my face in the icy wind. Underfoot I sank into the sea-soaked sand, making very slow progress, but determined to stay upright despite the wind and my plodding steps. Dressed in jeans, a blue and green weatherproof jacket and walking boots, I could have been any hiker enjoying the mild February Donegal weather. But I was not a passer-by, a blow-in delighting in this county's barren brown and green landscape, its picturesque sandy beaches and roaring seas. I knew this beach and town land, its lanes and fields and boulder-covered mountains. Drawing in breath, both physically and spiritually, I stood a moment, turning my greying head to gaze at the frothing sea. I felt good. It had been many years since I left, but I had returned often for short holidays. This time it would be for good. Not in the permanent sense of living here but there would be no more searching or travelling or doing. Here I would remain in spirit.

The clouds, gathering slowly, streaks of white against a soft blue, hastened me to the stony northern shore. A black and white collie stuck his nose over the grassy dune. When he began to running towards me I quickened my pace, not knowing whether the approach was friendly or aggressive. Glancing to my side I saw the dog slow to a trot, sniffing the air. I noted the cut above the eye, and wondered was it a fight or had it gotten caught on barbed wire? The animal seemed friendly, ran alongside me for a few metres, sniffed again and was over the sand dune before I knew.

Having eyed my rocky outcrop to sit upon I strode faster. A few drops of rain touched my sun-hardened cheeks. I grabbed the edges of the seaweed covered granite, but slipped and jarred my right hand between two jagged clefts of stone. Cursing inwardly I realised how hungry I was and my stomach gurgled its agreement. Despite my mishap and hunger I climbed upon my energy-giving rock and drank in the sight before me.

Breakfast was the usual holiday fare of bacon, sausage, potato bread, egg and toast. The freshly cut bread would toast well in the gas grill. I was getting hungrier, having only had a glass of water before leaving for

A Bump on the Road

my walk. I had rented a self-catering whitewashed cottage in a holiday village set up on the hillside. The previous occupants had gone, leaving a Christmas tree with decorations in one of the cupboards.

The three other cottages were deserted, separated from each other by little streams and bridges. Several horse-drawn hoes decorated the central yard, black and rusting. From the flagstone kitchen I could look out through the tiny nylon-curtained window the sea-edged land falling away where the sea dominated the view on three sides. Modern bungalows sat along the winding lanes leading to a harbour, amidst the boulder and rock-walled hedges of the green fields below. Above the harbour an ancient fort perched on the headland to the left. On the road up to the holiday village, a grotto to the Virgin Mary elevated on the hillside, newly tidied with a little paved area leading to the statue. Turning space was dug into the hill for a car. Behind the village the sheep-dotted mossy mountain rose steeply, a waterfall cascaded through the heather and bracken.

I had forsaken the many and various bed and breakfasts that hung their boards around every corner. Even the well-appointed hotels were closing down for their quiet season. I sought solitude after a life packed with people, places and movement. My laptop stored in the boot of the car, not to be booted under any circumstances. I had noted that the brochure described the holiday village as 'internet-aware' and thought momentarily of finding other accommodation but the off-season price included full-central heating, as much turf to burn as required, and a fridge full of food, some Guinness and a bottle of Jameson when booked over the internet. The fact that my booking came from Wellington, New Zealand, had aroused an even greater welcome from the manager of the village, John Gallagher, who had taught there for a few years in the eighties. Privacy was assured; there was enough food and drink in the house to last a couple of weeks. John would leave fresh milk and bread on the windowsill every three days and his phone number was on the Welcome Pack beside the telephone, should I require assistance or a bit of craic and a Guinness in the local pub.

A Bump on the Road

I visited these parts frequently, at least every couple of years, usually for a week or two. Now that my parents were dead there was little reason to stay other than a holiday to renew the spirit. My parents too, had returned here, natives after years in London and New York. My mother had returned and found she was pregnant with me, a late one that had the locals abuzz with excitement. I grew up here but, like my parents left when barely twenty, not unusual in those days. I still don't know why they returned here, perhaps, like me, they needed to close the door on the world. My father always said 'your mother brought me here', but he escaped into his books and music.

I studied my scraped hand, licking my wound. It was here, on these rocks that I renewed my spirit, a form of pilgrimage, home. Tears always welled up, I couldn't stop them. The wind died, tranquil, gulls disappeared, the clouds immobile as the beach brightened in weak sunlight. A sense of silence and surety always descended. Destiny assured. Inwardly, my clarity of mind made all possible, a fullness overtook me, yet I felt light and at ease. Around me an aura, shadows of persons I knew and didn't know. I felt very comfortable in this stillness. It had happened every time, since I was twelve. What only seemed a few minutes was in fact almost an hour. I knew this because I had missed the school bus that day. I told no one. I had been on my own that early morning to fetch some cattle from the shore before school. After it happened, I called it 'The Deliverance of Destiny', named in Western parlance after a movie I had seen.

These were the rocks of our childhood. Darting, carved wooden rifle in hand, leaping over the stone walls and grassy dunes, shooting the imaginary bad guys. The rifle had been carefully carved one summer holiday. My grandfather gave me an old penknife, ebony covered and cracked. It had been used for years for cleaning his well-worn pipe. The thin blade was now sharpened on the stone walls. The enemy was often a younger friend; we'd played together for years, climbing mountains, jumping streams and trudging muddy fields.

I had visited Ireland a few times since my parents died. I'd fly into Dublin and either visit the west or meet some old colleagues now

A Bump on the Road

working in the city. I'd always hired a car and travelled up north to walk this part of the beach. By simply being here, I could recharge my being. This time I had flown into Belfast and drove directly to the cottage. Perhaps I needed an instant recharge. Having arrived last night, I now sat on the potent rock. I believed the energy came directly from the earth and the lives lived before. The spirits of the people that went before – the farmers, the fishermen, those that died here, those that left, their forced emigration, their emotional energy left an indelible mark, forever present in the trees, in the rocks, in the ploughed soil, in the outcrop on which I sat. However, whether it was the seaweed-veiled rock on the beach or simply the benefits of a relaxing walk, I felt totally refreshed.
I left the strand via the tractor track on the northern edge, catching sight of used nappies and plastic bags caught in the pools and crevices of the rocky shore - the next sandy inlet was a mile away. I passed a rusting sign prohibiting the removal of sand from the beach, but judging by the state of the grassy track, things hadn't changed. A fifteen-minute walk took me to a walled field, now holding a hay-filled dilapidated building - my family home.

I jumped the tied gate into the original garden. The remnants of a privet hedge bordered a grassy rectangle and two climbing roses crept over the corner of the living room window. A boarded front door greeted me, instead of my mother, yet I could imagine her standing there, almost real. Hay was stored now where I had once dreamt of dragons, flying boats, beautiful princesses and foreign shores.

My grandparents lived in a small holding, two fields away, a few cows, a few sheep and a tiny shop which had supported at one time a family of eleven. They were more fortunate than many. My grandfather had been a Republican, a member of Irish Republican Army, the IRA. A balding man, when not farming, he drove a steamroller for the local council. When the local Member of Parliament got a concession to upgrade the roads in this area because the government of the day needed his vote, my grandfather's guaranteed income from smoothing the roads made life easier for his family.

A Bump on the Road

Unfortunately the good times evaporated as quickly as they had arrived. The contracts ended, and for a few months every year he got work on major projects, staying overnight in camps. Drink-talking resulted in fights. Luckily for him he had befriended a few saner blokes and they looked after each other.

He had never supported the drawing of the border. Like many colonial civil wars, families and friends were divided and rough justice was meted out to friend and foe. One night, his wife, himself and some of the younger members of the family left for Manchester, following the eldest son who had gone there. The farm was left in the hands of a nephew. In England, he quickly found work on the local council, driving a steamroller once more.

In my childhood I discovered why they had left in a hurry. One of his more unsavoury jobs with the IRA had been to execute an informer within the ranks. His baldhead was hidden permanently under his hat. An unshaven smooth face and soft eyes, soiled overalls and his wired-haired terrier by his side, he sat on a potato sack covered box in the shed, drawing on his pipe which was permanently hooked onto his lip, lit or unlit. His regime of cutting, scraping and tapping the tobacco into his pipe was perfected into a form of relaxation. With pipe and bottle of stout procured from somewhere, he told us stories of his flying column days - tales of gunrunning and hiding rag-covered revolvers in bridges. This particular story of his quick exit to England involved his selection as gunman to exterminate the suspected spy.

He was summoned to a local meeting of his group, drew the short straw and was told where to pick up a revolver. The spy was known to cycle home at a certain time. Cycling to the spot, he hid his bicycle under a hedge and positioned himself with a view of the road. He said he had never been so terrified in all his life and his clothes stank with fear and sweat. At one point he thought the game was up when a patrol of soldiers came by and paused at the very site. He was so close he could hear them laughing and smell their cigarette smoke. They moved on as he sank as close to the ground as possible. He stayed there, unmoving, until the early hours of the morning. Still, no target.

A Bump on the Road

After waiting for hours, he decided God was on his side so wrapped up the revolver and hid it in a culvert on a bridge. He was never so thankful. True or false, these stories forged a bond between our generations. Anyway, old comrades could quickly become enemies. The target and his family had disappeared shortly before an IRA unit was killed by a British ambush. An IRA investigation did not believe my grandfather when he told them the target had not turned up. Unknown to my grandfather someone had been sent to watch the execution from afar and stated he did not see my grandfather or the target. Did someone warn the target? They obviously suspected my grandfather. The result of this series of events - several IRA men died in a British ambush, the target disappeared and grandfather and his family were exiled to England.

A couple of nights later, John Gallagher rapped my window at ten thirty in the evening, a momentary jolt quickly give way to the realisation I was in Ireland. John invited me down to the local, a two-story house, the publican and family living above and behind the pub. Inside, the public bar looked like a kitchen from the fifties with a black range centrepiece - only a small bar in the corner and several tables gave it away. A huge dresser covered one wall, amassed with plates; holy pictures crowded the fire place. As we came in a young man in an Aran sweater finished off 'Homes of Donegal' in a reasonable voice. John whispered to me, "he's from Belfast, a blow in, wants us all to be back in the fifties."

I was introduced to a few locals who all knew my family, ready to chat but John and I quietly sat in the corner enjoying the pints. I think John worked out not to ask me too many questions but to simply be welcoming and offer a bit of company.

A burly man came in, yelling hello to everyone and I felt the slight tension in the atmosphere, as if my belt had tightened a notch. He had a chat with a few locals at the bar and then turned to stare at John and me. We ignored him for a while but after a few minutes I returned his gaze.

A Bump on the Road

"How are ye?"

"Well thanks," I replied

I went up to buy another round.

"So, you are McLaughlin, an' home on holidays. Having a good time?"

"I am."

"Good man."

I sat down with my drinks, feeling something had changed but the singer broke into song again, and by the time he finished we had nearly downed our pints, nice and smooth, worth coming out to the pub.

As we stood to open the door our burly friend came up to me.

"So your McLaughlin's grandson?"

"I am."

"Well, did you know my grandfather, his brother and a cousin died because of him?"

"Sorry to hear that," I said.

John nudged me to keep going. My accuser stood watching me from the doorway as we drove away.

"Don't worry about him, there's a few of them still living in the past," said John

"I'm not. I'm on my holidays."

A Bump on the Road

A Weak Tummy

Everything looked blatantly shiny and modern - the tartan-covered seats firm under buttock and the luminous walls gloriously stamped with the airline's motif. Its pungent chemical newness caught my breath. My stomach churned. Johnny took the window seat and elbowed me as the plane left the ground, the green fields and hamlets shrinking below. He liked peering through windows. A pack of ten cigarettes played in his hands already, waiting for the smoking sign to go on. He was as nervous as me.

Bing went the lighted sign and Johnny offered me a smoke, but I refused as my stomach was cramping one minute and feeling it needed evacuation the next. I knotted my sphincter muscle and closed my eyes, wishing away my time in the air. I was made aware of the confines of my seat once again, when the air stewardess prompted me with another boiled sweet before landing.

"Are you alright? You're as white as a ghost! Don't you boke here, for Christ's sake! Ach, is your wee tummy upset again?" He blew smoke over my face before it caught the exhaust draught and rose like a signal from an Indian camp fire. There was some comfort in Johnny empathetic self. His new blue floral shirt, the collar as wide as the airplane wings, and his denim jeans, ironed down the middle. Johnny liked to be neat in dress and everything else.

The plane steadied and I felt the colour returning to my face. My stomach relaxed but I refused the urge to have a smoke. Johnny was totally self-absorbed as usual, so I took the airplane magazine from the pouch in front of me. Within it a story on Manchester's night life - great bars to visit and soulful music venues. Unfortunately, I was going to a seat of learning two hours north of the city. What chance had I of getting to those splendorous places?
From the airport we got the bus to the city centre, arriving in Manchester's damp night air, and started looking for another bus to our hostel. Johnny spoke to one of the drivers and we dragged our suitcases over to the stop, hauled them onboard, and asked the driver to let us

A Bump on the Road

know when we'd reached our stops. He said there were other students on the bus too - a few pale pimply-faced youths sat behind their suitcases down the back, but we had to stand for the journey.

Johnny got off the bus first, about six stops before me, and I wished I was going with him. My mother had asked him to look after me as I was getting the bags out of the car boot. With great glee he reminded me of this every five minutes. A few others joined Johnny as they marched off into the dank evening. My stop. Several other lads walked with me to the hostel, little was said as we realised there were several hostels, side by side, aptly named Saint Patrick's Terrace, given the number of Irish lads arriving.

I walked up the steps and into the hall of my lodgings where a third-year student named Gerry was waiting. He was built like a rugby player, including the flattened nose, and introduced himself as such. His task was to help us settle into our new digs. He ticked my name off a list and showed me into the front room – an oversized, overused brocaded couch, some soft TV chairs and two long tables sat against the walls. Creamy wallpaper lined the room, devoid of any ornamentation, where a burning gas fire in a mottled green fireplace added to the stifling atmosphere. A sense of resignation hung in the air.

Of those gathered there, noticeably, a few were in their twenties, but all sat watching the television, turning round for a second when I came in. Gerry introduced me and they all said "hello" in unison, while maintaining their television-watching pose. Sitting on two dining chairs were two familiar faces from home, and not particularly welcoming ones, the Brown twins.

They had attended another school. I would sometimes meet them with a group of their mates on my way home, and, while they never physically hurt me, they would jostle, abuse and basically taunt the living daylights out of me. I tried to avoid them where possible, but my school mate, Larry, a younger version of Bryan Ferry, stood his ground and defiantly marched through them, almost willing them to touch him. I walked tightly in his wake. Giggling like two adolescent school girls were the twins, winking at me.

We were assigned rooms and my roommate turned out to be a local lad who told me he would go home every weekend. He didn't say much after that. I suppose it would be nice to have the room to myself at the weekends. It was a weird feeling leaving home for the first time, the security blanket removed. The unfamiliar room, the narrow metal bed, the hard sheets and the cool atmosphere kept me awake on my first night away from home – I was an alien. If my parents had come to collect me I would have gratefully gone back to their world.

Next morning, washing in the communal sinks and queuing for the odorous toilets, the sense of a world apart pervaded. However after a pleasant and warming breakfast we met the kindly hostel owner, Mrs. Polly, and Gerry informed us she made the tastiest food in the whole college. Her nourishing meals did make a difference. An army marches on its stomach, but homesick students need comfort food. The bus collected us for the institution that would carve our futures in the world of teaching. Gathering in the college's coffee shop I met Johnny and exchanged our first night experiences.

Eventually we were led to a lecture theatre to meet staff, and introductions were made. Groups wandered off to meet their subject coordinators, obtain timetables, reading lists and other requirements. Over the next few days we got organised for the start of lectures and tutorials the following week. The campus was small with classroom blocks, a cafeteria, and two tall, utilitarian, red-brick buildings reminiscent of Eastern Europe dominating its centre. A small, modern, cathedral-like chapel stood at the end of a long, snaking driveway. To its right a copse ran along a stream, while playing fields opened the vista on the other. Taking the public bus back to our hostels we entered the smoke-filled upper deck and lit up, exchanging wise cracks about our new lives as trainee teachers.

After dinner that night one of the older students, Alan, a lapsed trainee brother, suggested we sojourn to the local hostelry for a beer. It was a purpose-built public house, a block of pink stone with windows high

A Bump on the Road

under the roof line. To the left of the entrance was the public bar, to the right, the lounge, where we took residence, filling most of the corner. Buttoned brown leatherette benches lined two walls and a sequence of three interloping squares spread across the wallpaper above, matching squares in the browny-orange carpet littered with veneered tables and puffy stools. In the corner sat an organ on a small stage next to a hallway leading to the toilets – claustrophobic aridity. This was to be my welcoming local for the rest of the year.

I ordered a pint of mild – a soapy brew of drinkable cheapness. It gurgled within long after its last warm dreg. We got to know one another to a degree and soon identified likely drinking mates and possible friendships. The following days transmuted into weeks and soon struck a routine of dull lectures and classes, comforting food, and a drink in the evening after some television. Study was not strenuous and was certainly not the focus of our student life – how to socialise on the cheap.

On our daily trips to and fro, some neighbours recognised the contingent of Irish amongst the student body resident in Saint Patrick's Terrace. On one occasion when some of us were passing a garage in a laneway opposite, someone within yelled, 'Fuck off home, Paddies!' This was ignored by one and all. Our landlady told us that a couple of lads served in the army and were on leave. They worked on their cars in the laneway where we passed daily.

It was a Friday night, ideal for a pub crawl. Alan, our pack leader, rendezvoused with us in the hall for the engagement into the local drinking dens. Off we went into the chilly night for our inaugural night on the town.

The first sortie was a visit to The Fox and Hounds, a rundown rough spot where the men propped up the bar and not a female was in sight, except behind it. The floor looked unwashed and ashtrays overflowed onto the tables. We joked that we wouldn't be surprised if sawdust was on the floor or some fight was about to break out. Surprisingly, the beer tasted good. There was an air of menace. The barmaid was buxom and

A Bump on the Road

too friendly and, adding to our trepidation, she tugged Alan's ear every time she came to clear the empty pots, bending down so low that her bosom was almost in our pints. It didn't seem to occur to her to empty the heaving ashtrays.
The next stop was another modern version of what urban planners thought a public house should be, the Wet Whistle, a barn-sized room devoid of clients and atmosphere. We crowded round the juke box, playing a few pop tunes. The barman was visibly disappointed when we left.

Off we went up past Saint Patrick's Terrace to another, more sophisticated establishment. Plush red carpet embellished with golden winged horses, rich upholstered benches against the walls, overgrown stools circled dark wooden tables. Rows of upside down shimmering wineglasses hooked underneath glistening tankards hovered above a huge solid piece of dense mahogany. The mature and well-dressed clientele sipped at gin and tonics or foaming glasses of ale. Gloomy wood abounded, the walls splattered with brass plaques and scenes of bucolic villagers happily at work in their earnest livelihoods. A roaring fire was its finest attraction. The barman's steely service and the locals' stern glances threw a suspicious veil over our visit - we only stayed for one in the unfriendly Flying Horse.

Finally, we set off to our final pub for the night, our local, the Kilbeggan, its name betraying its Irish origins. Here we were sure of a welcome. The bar maids were getting to know us and knew we were a sociable bunch, if somewhat tight with our spending, but we caused no bother and happily spent our pennies.

I ordered my pint of mix and it immediately felt the wrong decision. My head and stomach were also in a bit of a mix, too much unfamiliar beer. At the bar a pleasant face stuck itself two inches from mine. Her sweet breath had a faint smell of gin, furthering my mixture of intoxication.

"I have been watching you all night. You look pretty young, but then I like them young," she smiled with a neat set of pale white teeth, remnants of spots covering her nose and cheeks. Her hair straggled over

A Bump on the Road

her ears and a fringe dropped over her eyes. They were tiny but I couldn't really see them anyway in my state of alcoholic brew. She had a crucifix tight around her neck. It was a nice neck, smooth and big enough to snuggle into there and then. I couldn't see the rest of her, as we were pushed together in the rush for last orders at the bar. Her forefinger stroked the back of my hand and asked,

"Will I see you tonight?"

"Why not?" I answered.

She pushed her way out of the crush and I saw her tightly packed jean-covered bum.

When I returned to my mates, they slagged me about the beauty I had been chatting up at the bar. "You quiet ones are always the same, still waters run deep!" A roar of forced laughter erupted from them and a couple of slaps on my back had me spilling my beer down my jacket. I didn't tell them she had done the chatting up. My guts were gurgling and my head swimming - surely I could finish my last pint with the lads. Yorkshire Alan struck up with 'On Ilkla Moor Baht 'at' and before long the entire lounge was engulfed in the unofficial anthem of his county. Most of us knew the verse but Alan sang all of it in the dialect, explaining afterwards that it meant being on the moor without a hat. Not to be outdone by the Yorkshire import, one of the locals kicked off with the football anthem 'You'll never walk alone', and sure enough the whole place rang again with our collective drunken voices.

It was enough for me. I went to the toilets to steady my head, but that wasn't sufficient, so I went outside. A few of the locals gathered at the door to say their goodnights before heading home. I didn't fancy being sick in front of them so wandered around the back to a lane and walked around a bit. I threw up, luckily missing my clothes, although my shoes got sparked. I felt a little more clear-headed and my stomach settled. I could do with drink of tea. After a few minutes I went back to the outside of the pub's door, hoping to catch the lads on their way home, and went over to a patch of grass to wipe my shoes.

A Bump on the Road

Suddenly, an arm locked around mine, and she with the appealing neck embraced me.

"Oh, you don't half stink of vomit. Come on, you can walk me home, it's not far."

She literally dragged me with her, her comment that she had been watching me all night kept rolling around in my befuddled head. Why would she want to kiss a mouth like mine? It felt like a dried out cesspool. She led me down some paths behind the houses.

"What's your name?" I asked.

"Paula."

She didn't ask my name but sensed my nervousness. "It's not far, just the end of this row." I was too confused to even ask what was happening, but I was beginning to sober up fast. I could hear running feet behind me, and my instincts registered danger. It was something I had learnt very early in life – run, and live to fight another day. I took to my heels, hoping they were behind me and not at the end of the lane. I heard someone roar, "We only want to talk to you, Paddy!" Not tonight.

I slipped into a side lane and kept off the main streets, watching, listening, waiting. Once I was sure they were not behind me, I tried to get my bearings. It all looked the same to me in the dark - rows of terraces and back alleys. Making my way onto the main street and up towards my house, I worried they would be waiting for me, ready to jump out from a side street or lane. There were a few back paths that led home, past the pub again, but I thought it best to stay on the main street where a few people were also heading home.

At last I reached the end of our street. It was dark, with mature trees masking the lights, and the wind in the leaves threw an eerie atmosphere

A Bump on the Road

over the road. I could run, but they might hear me. Perhaps they were watching, even now.

I was pushed from behind. My stomach somersaulted, but it was the Brown twins with a half dozen others, including the student rugby players.

"You're pissed," said one of the twins.

I didn't contradict him, and mumbled something, much relieved to meet them. I followed closely and thought of something to say to the biggest bloke there, a friendly Welsh front forward. I queried him about his school days and his playing experiences. He seemed really chuffed.

As we approached the entrance to our house, six men approached us, all crew cuts and tee shirts despite the chill weather.

"Hey, we want to talk to Paddy here," said one, putting his hand on my shoulder. My Welsh front forward stepped in front of me, pushing his arm off me.

No one spoke and we continued walking into our house, leaving the group standing outside.
"We only want to talk to wee Paddy!"

Later we told the publican of our local and never had any bother after that. He had a quiet word, and my Welsh front forward, Owen, and I became big buddies, frequently enjoying a few scoops together.

A Bump on the Road

So You're Off Then?

"So you're off then?" said Harry, dullness in his eyes and voice, holding his niece's hand. "Now, if Australia needs shirts, you know where to get them," he said to lighten the moment, kissing her wet cheeks. And then off they went, his niece and her husband, up the gangplank. The misty rain dripped from their noses despite their elaborate hats and bonnets. Family and friends were all dressed in their Sunday best, with many similar groups leaving their loved ones too. Meagre belongings in boxes and trunks already loaded on board. On deck, the two emigrants waved to their friends below and Harry waved back, leaving the group of well wishers behind to walk up the quay.

He walked along the river, pass the warehouses, the cranes and milling dock workers, inhaling the damp air and not looking back. He would miss his sister's daughter, but more so would miss his brother, his face set to betray little emotion. Harry could hear the band starting up again - the last passengers must have boarded. . Many locals came down to the riverside to see the emigrants off on their voyage, enjoying the emotional occasion. His brother, Paul and his young bride had stowed away below shortly before dawn. The boat, a packet steamer, was en route to Liverpool where they would board a ship.

Harry remembered the previous weeks and heard about the parties, where most of the farewells took place for his niece, and the night his brother Paul approached him. Harry's wife, Mary, and their children had said their goodbyes to the niece on the same night. People called these goodbyes 'wakes' but not Harry – he was sure he would see Paul again but suspected he would never see his niece again. Harry's mind started to spin but forced himself to focus on today's undertakings as he made his way to his office.

Harry Norman was a man of means, as they say here in town, a prosperous plumber, owning several houses, a carriage, a new car, a work truck and an employer of a dozen men. His new town residence, with the shop at the bottom, the workshop out the back and the two stories of family living above were his wife's pride and joy. It was his

A Bump on the Road

former employer's home, who, having no descendants, sold the successful business to the best apprentice he ever had.

Harry ran the business himself for years, his former boss becoming a silent partner, but his name was not over the shop front. Harry understood this was the only way, to maintain the existing customers and future ones, including the important and sizable contract with the local council. It was only on his employer's deathbed did the company become Harry's.

Harry and Mary renovated the house before moving the family into this prestigious address. The kitchen-living room on the second floor with its centerpiece, the latest Aga range. A scullery was off to the left. On the top floor, four sparely furnished bedrooms for the family of six - their three girls and one boy.

Pride of place was a newly refurbished front parlour, lined in embossed ochre wallpaper. The centerpiece, here, in the huge bay window overlooking the cathedral grounds opposite, was a mighty oak table, a silver candelabra sat in its centre. Matching chairs, recently recovered in earthy brocade, surrounded it and even more chairs stood against the walls. Hung from the ceiling, a silver and glass candelabra obtained from a local country mansion. On the black marble mantle, brass candlesticks and a brass and marble carriage clock sat above the dark green tiled fireplace, each tile slightly different, but all depicting embossed dancing nymphs in a glade. Around the hearth, a brass rail shone in unison with a rack of brass fire implements. Dried flowers in purple and spice dressed the grate, while a substantially stuffed brocaded sofa sat in front. A china cabinet arrayed with colourful plates and family photographs and within the newly purchased Staffordshire dinner china.

The two cabinets on the left of the fireplace were Mary's domain. Below, full of linen and tablecloths; above, through glass door another display of English china tea sets, coloured glass and crystal. On the right, the cupboards belonged to Harry and his business. Here he kept his ledgers, plumbing books and his own personal items.

A Bump on the Road

Under the heavily draped windows, on most nights, Harry retrieved his ledgers, adding to the figures from the dockets sent up from the shop below, or supplied by his foreman out on the various work sites. Mary helped, checking the numbers and planning the next day's work. This meeting became increasingly important, with Mary's input - she was helping to run the successful business. Harry and Mary had an marriage, almost arranged by Mary's mother, whose own ambition had helped make Mary's parents the owners of one of the most productive and wealthy farms in Donegal. The importance of networking and accessing influential people was a value bequeathed to her daughter Mary.

It was, after all, in the course of business that Mary's father noticed young Harry, his industry and astuteness, conspicuous amongst his peers. The marriage proved fertile in family and business. They had four healthy children, and they grew to love and respect one another, over the years.

Having a successful plumbing company, twelve employees and several houses was enough ambition for Harry. Mary, however, had more in her mind. She wanted an address in the right area, which she got, mixing and working with people of prominence and position. A part-time maid and cook allowed Mary to concentrate on the business and her children, and it was Mary's desire for self-improvement that led her children into the best schools.

She was an avid reader but wise enough not to expand on 'liberal' ideas in polite company and still be seen as the dutiful wife of Harry, the well-known prosperous business man. It was at these nightly planning sessions with Harry when Mary encouraged him to develop this relationship or that one. Her favourite saying was 'A hint to the wise is enough,' and this was true for Harry Norman. She found it hard to hide her pride when Harry's company won the contract to replace and extend the town water's supply and manhole covers bearing the Norman name appeared throughout the town centre's streets.

A Bump on the Road

Mary and Harry had moved home a few months ago, their previous larger house with its huge garden had a less upwardly mobile address. In those months, Mary got busy and joined committees of all hues: working-men's libraries, church and charity groups, a temperance association, and even St. Patrick's Cathedral Garden Committee, a church not of the Norman's religion. She was an enthusiastic member and made welcome, indeed her membership was the talk of the Church of Ireland. After she joined a sub-committee of the Garden Committee was formed, ostensibly to supply flowers for the services, the fact it duplicated the work of her committee did not bother her at all - it was all networking.

Mary lived opposite the fifteenth century cathedral. To the east lay a small graveyard for some of its ministers and a few bishops, but, more importantly for Mary, it was a landscape of controlled grandeur behind the safety of the railings – majestic oak trees, trimmed grass, stony paths, overflowing flowerbeds, and wooden benches – unused and kept immaculate. All could be viewed from Mary's front room.

One evening, after a meeting at the cathedral, one of the ladies, Mrs. Jennet drew her aside.

"I was wondering Mary, if you could oblige us. My husband's group are laying a wreath at the War Memorial and marching back here for a service. They want to take off their overcoats before going into the cathedral. Thousands of the visitors to the service will use the cloakroom and hall in the cathedral. It would great if we could find a place for their coats. Sure, you are one of our own, so could they leave them at your house. It would be an ideal place." Mary could not refuse and her front parlour was a cloakroom for the orange men's parade.

Any friction with her own church over her membership at Saint Patrick's Cathedral was solved by increasing her weekly donation and reducing her husband's fee for all the plumbing maintenance at her local church, St. Kevin's. The imposing Italianate altar, a substantial shrine in white marble depicted the story of St. Columba in blue and gold mosaic frescos. After all, it was Harry that organised the Dockers to defend the church and school, when riots broke out after one of the traditional marches, resulting in roaming mobs attacking anything that smelt of Rome.

The Norman's, now leading members of their church and local community, were also instrumental in helping the Christian Brothers settle in the town. Three new Christian Brothers arrived and stayed in one of Harry's houses, free of charge. Little did they know that many of the clothes and knitted jumpers supplied to them, via Mary, came from the Church of Ireland's congregation. This was a sound business investment, whenever the Brother's home or school needed any plumbing, it was Harry who got the contract.

Most of the committees' leaders were women like Mary - strong, determined, ambitious, and influential in their homes, committees and husbands' businesses but not public figures themselves. They were often the power behind the masculine throne. Education, self-improvement and networking were the way forward. Even so, they had to be careful, as many of their peers saw their duty purely in the service of their husband and God. Through her noble work, Mary met the charitable ladies. Their wealth allowed them maids and housekeepers, and thus, with time and money on their hands, the women set about improving their lot and their community.

The current vogue was indoor bathrooms, and so with Mary's light touch, Harry had a schedule of installing and updating bathrooms for at least a year in advance - doing the privies for the well heeled. The move to Cathedral Street had already advanced herself and her husband, professionally and socially, at least in her mind.

Harry's elder brother, Paul, was a bit of a dreamer. Mary said he had no sense of industry or ambition, not a practical man. His real passion was music. A talented pianist, he played and taught music, living at home on the farm until his mother died. With the family gone and their father dead, their mother rented out the fields. Helping with the remaining chickens was about as much as Paul could offer, his mother said his singing in the chook shed helped them lay the biggest eggs in the county.

As the eldest brother, and the last on the farm, the farm was traditionally his, but Paul was happy to sell up and spilt the monies with his family. His sisters were married and well settled with their own families. After their mother died, Harry had fulfilled his familial duty by welcoming Paul into Cathedral Street. Paul's charming etiquette and love of reading, often absenting himself to his room, and his eagerness to tutor the children fostered genuine warmth with Mary. The lack of a piano in the house hindered his tutoring profession, making the situation all the more temporary. Mary would have loved a music room, another sign of liberal advancement, but there just wasn't enough room. Her previous home had a piano and the family renting it from the Normans allowed Paul to use it for practice and tutoring, in return for tutoring their own children. However, it was on the wrong side of town for the city's developing middle-class, and their current fashion for installing pianos (and new bathrooms) helped alleviate the need for tutoring outside their homes.

The tradition of music and dance permeated the fabric of the city - singing, dancing, and playing music was as natural as the continual damp. It was the accepted norm for children to learn an instrument or to partake in some sort of singing group. Some even participated in the yearly pantomime. Most families had somebody learning the piano.

Paul needed a property, but there were none available to him. He was encouraged to buy in the vicinity of Harry's old house but Paul wanted something more central and anyway given the times, it was difficult to obtain property for people of his religion. In the mean time, he would have to stay at Cathedral Street.

Paul's business prospered. He even became a demonstrator for a music store, his natural talent allowed him to lift any instrument and demonstrate it to customers – the guitar, a trumpet, already a competent player on the fiddle and a few others. It was a short walk from his

A Bump on the Road

lodgings, and he was called in to demonstrate, as necessary. Fortunately, a back room was also available for tutoring.

Outside the premises, a manhole cover with his surname acted as a doormat. The owner encouraged Paul to practice as much as he liked, fondly referring to some of the more dramatic pieces as his favourites, knowing it attracted customers.

On such an occasion, on hearing the music, the Duke of Knockavoe came in, wanting to inspect some pianos. He already had a Steinway in his music room but his children used a Broadwood. It was his daughter's Diana's eighteenth birthday, already an accomplished pianist and she had asked for her own piano. Paul was playing Beethoven's Fifth Symphony opening the bars with weighty treatment, and the Duke recognised its four-note motif. After conversing with owner of the music store, he approached Paul.

"That is a wonderful sound, my good man, one of my favourite pieces. I believe you do a spot of tutoring? My daughter needs a new tutor, her previous chap passed away, nice fellow, a bit deaf. What about it then?"

"Yes, indeed I do, when would it suit?"

"Oh, I leave all that to my dear wife, brilliant organiser, don't know where I'd be without her. Have you a phone number? I'll tell you what. Francis, my wife is coming to see one of these blessed piano things on Saturday afternoon, talk to her then! How's that? Lovely to talk to you, and I just love your playing. Play on! Bye." He called back to the owner who stood within hearing distance, "My wife will see you on Saturday." as he strode out.

On returning to Cathedral Street, over dinner, Paul told Mary and Harry about his encounter with the Duke and his prospective employment. Mary immediately rose and offered Paul another piece of roast beef. "Tell us more," as she placed it on his plate, not waiting to see if it was wanted. She also offered their car to take him to the Duke's castle, a Crossley Torquay that barely left the garage, except to sit outside the

A Bump on the Road

house when visitors came or a few Sunday runs. Harry's eyes widened but he remained silent.

Having made arrangements with the Duke's wife, Paul drove to the estate, an elegant castle dating from the thirteen century. He parked in the central courtyard, just outside the music room on the ground floor.

His student, Diana was a demure eighteen year old with whom he immediately fell in love. She had an appetite for knowledge, an enchanting sponge. Subdued, and withdrawn at first, but relaxed and more talkative as the weeks went by. They would talk and talk about their interests - music, the countryside, animals, literature, art, cities, far away countries and the possibility of travel. He described, in detail, his weekly drive to her - the cottages, the local inhabitants, the oak trees, the native flowers and of course, the seasonal weather.

Paul made the sun shine for Diana, no matter what the weather was like. It awoke the possibility of another life, the freedom to travel, to do what she wanted, to study art and architecture in Rome and Paris or by the canals of Venice. Paul brought his books on art and European cities with him for her to study. Diana convinced her mother to let Harry tutor her younger sister, Beatrice, so Paul came twice a week. His love for Diana grew, not for any sexual gratification but as a master to a student. He guided that thirst for knowledge and desire for learning, and loved every minute of it. They would go for walks through the estate with Beatrice as chaperone. He was falling deeper in love.

During one tutoring session Diana happened to mention they were getting the bathroom updated in the children's wing and that she had to wash in cold water the last few mornings. The plumbers were from England and had to return for health and family reasons.

Over dinner in Cathedral Street, after each visit to the estate, Mary wanted detailed information about the gardens and the rooms. She encouraged him to ask for a tour of the house and asserted that he should pay attention to the furnishings and not the silly old stuff on the walls or the date of this or that, as Paul would sometimes ramble about.

A Bump on the Road

When he mentioned that they had plumbing problems in the castle, Mary immediately offered another slice of meat. Harry could see where this was going, but said nothing. Mary suggested their plumbing company could help, if they were stuck. Therefore, after the next lesson Paul asked to see Diana's mother.

Diana went off to see her mother and, upon returning, took Paul to a sitting room, thick with couches and drapes. This was their winter night's sitting room, cozy and warm. After a half an hour, The Duchess arrived, and Paul explained his brother's business. She asked if Harry could call the next day.

After seeing the Duchess and consulting with the estate's manager, Harry got the job to finish off the bathroom in the children's wing. Mary was beside herself. They now had the Duke of Knockavoe as their most prestigious customer.

After one of her meetings in the cathedral, the Deacon stopped Mary to talk, and asked about the job with the Duke. Mary's mouth dropped open but she caught it before he noticed, a skill she had learnt a long time ago to maintain facial impassivity at all times. The Bishop had told her that he had given a reference for Harry.

A few weeks later, The Duke summoned Harry to the castle and discussed further plumbing needs - bathrooms, water supply and heating requirements. Could they come to some arrangement in a couple of month's time? Harry chuckled at Mary's reaction, "Calm yourself, dear, you're fit to be tied."

A couple of months later, on a close autumnal Sunday evening, Harry suggested they join the Ramblas. The nights had been drawing in fast, but it was stuffy in the house. Most young local couples promenaded through the town and down the hill towards the bridge on a Sunday evening. It was not something Mary would do, much preferred a trip in their car and a walk along the northern coastal resorts. A short walk would be nice though, so she pulled a cape over her shoulders, fixing her hair and face. The Normans joined the throng for the evening's

A Bump on the Road

downhill canter. They walked passed the cathedral and into the main shopping street, from here they could see the spires from St. Kevin's and the cathedral. Walking down the hill they passed several shirt factories, the three largest in the town, the five story edifice at the bridge, one of the biggest in the world. Harry enjoyed the spectacle of industry and recreation and church.

Thankfully, Mary thought, they didn't have to stand and talk with anyone, just the cursory "lovely evening" to everyone. Harry dismissed the nagging thoughts from his mind, his waistcoat tight across his chest, happy with his fortune in his town. Was he about to embark on his most prestigious project yet? Though he worried about how much profit it would make. He quietly told a revered colleague at the last Plumber's Guild meeting in Belfast, who whispered back, "I hope they pay you, they have a reputation!"

On their return, a crowd was gathered at their front door, a small army of policemen and in the centre, the Duke, banging his walking stick on Harry's door.

"Where is he? Where is he? The blackguard, I'll wring his bloody neck. He has eloped with Diana. I found her note." His face reddened as he lifted his walking stick high in the air. Mary stepped behind her husband grabbing the rear of his coat with both hands.

A Bump on the Road

New Neighbour

If this is suburbia, I'll drink to it: sitting on a tree stump, drinking deep drafts of a cold beer, and watching the hypnotic sway of the see-through eucalypt, its branches forming a near perfect semi-circle against the sheet blue sky. The tree stump marked one of the corners of a once-neat vegetable garden; on the other corner stood the red-brick barbecue under a canopy of ivy, its cooking surfaces black and rusting, flecks of grease still embedded in every crevasse. Moving into the barbecue's green-clad shelter to escape the intense heat, I stretched my sun-starved legs into its rays, my heels amidst the scurrying ants on the bleached earth.

My bumptious landlord had just left; cheerful because I had paid him six months' rent in advance, a price to ensure tenancy and a roof over my head in this anonymous suburb. He quibbled over my references but was convinced with my cash offer and beamed, "I like Irish, I love your accent! You drink, you Irish always drink and fight. No fights, we be friends! I bring over a nice cold Aussie beer for you, my friend. That good, eh? That good", I replied. He arrived in the driveway in his bashed Ute, a black mongrel yapping on the back, amidst fridges, pipes and a green settee populated with red roses. He insisted on taking me on a tour of the post Second World War bungalow for the third time, extolling the many features he had updated: the modern bathroom, the central heating, the newly painted walls. Saving the best to the last, he pointed to the 1962 gas cooker. Yes, the gas cooker with its warming oven up top, just perfect for keeping a man's meal warm of an evening, just the thing for making an evening glow with success.

As we toured the garden, he introduced me to yet another Aussie icon, the Hills Hoist. A clothes line: just the thing for the stay-at-home Mum, standing proud beside her newly washed clothes. The premier of all clothes lines, spinning gently in the breeze while the dinner is cooking on the gas stove and the plates are warming in the little oven above. Idyllic suburban living.

A Bump on the Road

The landlord arrived with a chilled six-pack. I refused to take one until he left, enjoying the cold liquid and warm sky, looking at the see-through tree - a welcome relief after his forced bon ami. It had obviously been a neat and productive garden to satiate the eyes and stomachs of the previous occupants. The triangular circle of the Hills Hoist dominated the garden, its position dictated by the path of the sun, screened slightly by a privet hedge. I could see them in the nearby gardens, disused and disorderly, their once taut lines; a proud cobweb, now dilapidated and hanging forlornly.

I sat perched supping the blue sky, the cold beer and the mesmeric branches.

Needing a newspaper to look for a job I went down to the shopping strip - a row of rusting overhangs protecting the customer from the extremes of the weather. Each displayed garish neon advertising, contrasting with the cute Heritage Green and Dickensian shop fronts of the old world. This world of light and warmth dictating various modes of American-style architecture, yet distinctly Australian, softened with a string of shady trees, perhaps to hide the mistaken folly of such commercialism. The road was awash with traffic islands, forcing transient cars to slow their onward journeys. In the newsagent, tier upon tier, parades of magazines, stacked with beckoning expertise, everything from gardening to yachting. World newspapers sat beside natives. In the lottery corner colourful instructions announced their confident message: 'it could be you!' You too could become a millionaire for a few bucks and a little luck. The fact that you needed heaps of luck and more than a few bucks was silently ignored. I picked up the tabloid; the front page showed a smiling, buxom blond. The other broadsheets seemed just too serious. The grinning shopkeeper wished me "G'day" and seeing my fumbling with the new coinage, kindly helped himself to the contents of my palm. "See you later," he said, still smiling. Had he taken more than necessary?

The short walk home took me up a hill past a 1960s school and church with a Virgin Mary grotto decorated with flowers and small branches of, I guessed, native trees. The church front; a wall of frosted windows and

A Bump on the Road

neat green lawns, the school; a wall of redbrick and a row of canopied windows of wooden Venetian blinds, its path weaving around the main building to more rooms for educational entertainment.

At the foot of the slope was a garage, clean and neat. Above it, curiously, sat a bungalow, screened with lattice and encrusted with red and purple flowers. The cleanliness struck me as odd, reminiscent of a 1950s black-and-white American film: a town taken over by aliens but everything still appearing perfectly normal. A radiant Ford Popular, 1956 on its number plate, was proudly displayed in the gleaming showroom window. As I looked at the car I nearly tripped over an elderly lady walking slowly in front of me.

She was bent slightly forward; her rather large bottom had pink knickers sneaking out from under her brown trousers. A chocolate brown cardigan rose from above the knickers to her grey, sharply cut hair, highlighting a small, bulbous nose and a sagging chin pointed towards the opposite side of the road. Her interest was taken by the renovations of a 1930s Californian bungalow. The roof was off, exposing rafters and a new second story added with modern straight lines, where three men in shorts, bareback, exposed in the Australian sun worked on the new addition. Was it the muscular, bee-like activity that attracted her attention or did she still like to see a bit of bronzed flesh? At the end of her arms, several plastic bags hung from each hand, tipping my lady forward. I was scarcely aware of the situation unfolding in front of me; it took a second to dash in an effort to stop her from falling onto the ground. She tripped over a hole in the pavement and landed hard on her side, banging her head. I was met with a thud and the contents of the bags, beans and bottles, rolling under my feet.

Unthinkingly, I began to pick them up, but then flung them on the grass verge and said, "How are you, would you like me to lift you?"

"No," came the sharp answer. I let her lie there, and put a bag of flour under her head. I asked again a few minutes later, and she agreed, so I helped her into a sitting position. "That'll do," she said. "I'll sit here awhile to catch my breath." I thought, this is a sensible lady, unashamed

A Bump on the Road

to sit on the pavement. If it had been my mother she would have jumped up and run home, collapsing in a heap with pain and embarrassment. A few people gathered around but moved on when I said I would take her home. I helped her to her feet and she sat on a low wall, a slight cut on her left temple. I picked up her groceries and she announced she would go home. Carrying her bags, we walked in silence until we turned the corner to my street. With a wan smile she told me she lived here too. Having passed my house, she stopped at the driveway next door and identified it as her home. I informed her that I was to be her new neighbour and escorted her into her kitchen, where she sat on a kitchen chair while I prepared some tea.

"I'm leaving in a month or so to visit my daughter in Tasmania. She's worried I'm getting too old to look after myself. I have a weak heart and it's not getting better. And this house is falling down," she said.

Sure enough, it was ready for the beauties from the building site to attack it with vigour and modern ideas. I smiled as I gave her the tea; she was slumped on the chair. Bertha had a shaky drink from the mug and continued.

"I am going to look at a little cottage a mile away from my daughter, she lives in the boondocks. I always like to wander down to the shops and have a chat with someone. There is always someone to chat to. If I like it, I'll sell up and move down. With the price of houses nowadays I should make a pretty penny."

I told her my name and we discussed a shortened and sanitised history of my life. After our tea, I gave her my new phone number and left her using a walking stick to go to bed. As I was leaving by the back door, I called to her to have a phone by her bedside. She replied that she already had. Her back garden had all the same ingredients as mine, but was overgrown. At the end of a path down the side of the grass stood her own Hills Hoist, its lines sagging with use.

Five minutes later, my phone rang. It was Bertha, and she didn't feel well and was dizzy. "What is the emergency number?" I asked. "Is it

116

A Bump on the Road

triple zero?" I phoned the ambulance and we were inside it on the way to hospital soon after. She was very concerned she was causing me bother, but I told her it was OK, I had nothing important to do anyway.

I wanted to chat to her but wasn't sure if I should. The monitors had been placed on her, and she seemed well and was smiling, so I asked about her childhood. She had been born in Melbourne, the daughter of taxi driver – a horse and coach. The horse was stabled in the back yard of a small cottage in Fitzroy. Her childhood was uneventful; she had kind parents and two siblings, all of them now dead. Her daughter lived in Tasmania, a doctor and an active member of the Greens, looking to escape the ravages of consumerism. Bertha was involved in politics, always supporting the workers to improve their working conditions, always on the march and ready to lend her support to any worthy cause. On one of these marches she had met her husband, Ben, a journalist. They married and lived in her parents' house, but redevelopment and three children moved them to her current home. They made many additions to the house, but all that stopped when Ben was knocked down one morning on the way to the train. He survived for two days. Bertha got a job working in the office of a local paper and eventually did some journalism too.

After arriving at the hospital, she was examined and I asked if she wanted me to wait. She seemed weaker, so I said I would contact someone, her daughter perhaps, or one of her other children, but Bertha said she would phone them after the tests. A doctor came out to me in the waiting room and said they would do a scan, but that everything seemed to be OK, and I could go in and sit with her. She was pale but in good form. I kicked off the conversation by asking her if she got any interesting stories as a journalist. With her interest in politics and her quick brain, she had managed to become one of their political correspondents, often when a lady was required.

"Not many men would talk to you in those days, even off the record. I got the softer things, like when the Premier opened schools and hospitals, or when their wives attended functions, flower shows and the like."

A Bump on the Road

"Surely you must have picked up titbits or inside info?"

She looked at me and for the first time her eyes twinkled. She chuckled and lifted her arms up automatically, but, remembering she was unwell on a hospital bed, she dropped them again slowly. For a moment she was back in those heady days.

"I had a few stories to tell, still have in fact, but they were never fully told. Scams, corruption, infidelity, even murder, but most of it was just little nuggets. Put them together and we got a story, but nine times out of ten before we got the full story, something happened. The pollie resigned due to health reasons, or was sacked, or things got settled quietly. I reported to the Chief Correspondent, he took most of the credit for my donkey work, but that's the way it was in those days. It took years before my name was credited to a piece."

"Did you ever get the full story?" I asked.

"Once or twice. Expense claims that were pure fiction, that led back to brothels or investment properties, or odd transactions in bank accounts. Most of it was donkey work, a lot of it, but there was good fun too. I would be taken out for a meal and asked to bury a piece. One guy even offered to marry me! Well, I laughed so loud, the other diners looked round. He turned beetroot red. I knew, everyone knew, he was gay, but not the public. He was looking for a female escort for the public to see. Lots of boring stuff too! The one that got me jailed for refusing to name my sources was fun. I was only working on it for a few days, but they tried to frighten me off. The Leader of the Opposition's daughter was sleeping with a Russian based in Canberra."

The curtains drew back and a doctor appeared. I was asked to leave. They were taking Bertha for a scan. I had so many questions to ask. I held her hand for a second as the trolley went by.

"Good luck, I am going to enjoy living beside you." She smiled and the eyes brightened again. "I'll wait," I shouted, as her trolley went through

A Bump on the Road

the doors to the examination room. I had only met this lady a couple of hours ago and yet I felt as if I'd known her all my life.

Thirty minutes later a doctor came to find me and took me into an office. There had been complications. Bertha had a brain haemorrhage, coupled with a weak heart she had passed away. The doctor told me to wait there. I felt numb, unable to speak or feel anything; I wandered, shocked, out of the hospital, walked to a train station, and worked out the two trains that took me home. I was alive but it seemed as if my stomach had a hole in it, there was just nothing there, yet I felt as if I had eaten a heavy meal and could throw up. There were no thoughts, no understanding, just instinct telling me to go home. My back door was still open when I arrived, an empty house. I went to the fridge and took a beer from my landlord's six-pack. With the cool can in my hand, I found the stump and sat once again contemplating the comforting sight of the Hills Hoist.

A Bump on the Road

Down Memory Lane

Dreaming of lives past, present and future might be an appropriate place to start. Growing up in a small, Irish town, what was real and concrete, memories metamorphosing, susceptible to time and mood or reality? Travelling back to pick the earliest memories for recollection confuses even further. Did it happen? Did it happen like that? Does it really matter? Family, education, culture, community - formed the roots that spiral to the present. Memories and dreams collide in a fusion of unreality, yet real, as if it happened yesterday, a flow of motion - emotion.

Small touchstones, such as: holding on to the cream twin-tub washing machine, vibrating metal against skin - sexual, sensual, memories of tangible embrace. Happy emotions project through time, holding with trance-like immediacy - a meditation, pent-up energy of life, transient and momentary. The spin drier - its aluminium blue lid and turquoise bulbous edging, yellow kitchen cupboards, melamine yellow table and matching marble bench tops, floor littered with neat piles of divided laundry; whites, coloureds, socks and underwear, shirts. My job was to green-soap my father's shirt collars and cuffs. Once all the piles were hung out, the twin tub's lid was replaced and put away in the cupboard, all shone up.

Everything shining - table, cooker, sink and ornaments. Reality shone, shut away, behind the doors and curtains. Important to keep the dross enclosed in lace curtains at front and nylon ones at the back, fresh paint yearly at the front of the house, every three years at the back.

The sitting room, darkened by thick curtains, seemed a mysterious place reserved for visitors - priests, relatives, neighbours and various dignitaries. Some aunts charged on through to the back rooms, the kitchen and dining room with a battered brocaded couch and television in the corner. This is where Robin Hood projected his weave of greenery and goodness every Saturday, 'Loved by the good, feared by the bad, Robin Hood, Robin Hood'. Into the rain-bowed sun showers we leapt, with swords in hand, carefully pared and tapered by kitchen

A Bump on the Road

knives, with cross bar nailed haphazardly. Filled with such high positive energy we danced with balletic finesse in sword fight. Stick-battered thumps and fingers didn't affect us, just like Robin and his men. Moments, past, present, fuse together and fade into past once more.

Memories and the realities of life fade and come closer with abrupt poignancy. A smell, perhaps, the mossy moistness damp after a shower of rain. The wet dripping from my duffle coat onto rain-logged trousers of past walks home after school. Intense memories of past: oft - repeated habits, overpowering. A previous time, past the huge, noisy security gates of the nearby factory, lorries to-ing and fro-ing, blue frocked men jumping from cabs shouting greetings to the friendly gate men who lazily saunter to check the documents. Payroll security vans whizzing through, alert eyes and stiff countenances, uncomfortable. Once, a security van's windscreen was smashed, glass mosaics scattered on pavement and bonnet - men in uniform swarming around, nodding, some laughing, others directing traffic, the van's front wheels half on the pavement and kerb. Excitement flooded as I looked on, real life impinging on dull routine. I moved closer to the van and looked into the driver's seat plotted with blood. A flash and two days later my two tone brown and beige cardigan fronted not just the local paper but also a national British daily. Real life - it was great.

More mundane but captivating memories from those early days - I still sense the damp smell of those places. The main road, a different world unfolds, large detached houses, one with an English mopping thatched roof. Another country, another town, a picturesque English village, treed, wide, traffic going somewhere, different from the inbred culture I knew, the possibility of another life from my own. The smell of freshly baked bread, promises of time travel, instantaneously back to being a six-year-old child. Smells and atmospheres do that to people. Of course, in childhood memories, the sun seemed to shine, yellow like custard, mixed with apprehension and joy. Custard - Bird's custard. School custard wasn't stodgy like yellow porridge, but thin, smooth, flowing. I was encouraged to eat it by my teacher, followed by tea and biscuits. I was a sickly child.

A Bump on the Road

My primary education was fed intellectually by a warrior class; thumped, battered and bruised for my own benefit - educationally and spiritually. We were young soldiers of the church and of Ireland. Female teachers came from a similar class. One fellow pupil got bounced off walls and strapped more often than the rest of us, but then it was his father who taught us.

There were gentle giants too: the tall lady dressed in black, letting us play in her make believe shop at the back of her classroom. The other: small, greying, teacher- pads at elbows, small check shirt, shuffling figure with a friendly aged face, came from out of town, spreading magic amidst the stones. A bump on the road, says he, that's where I am. He allowed us to go to the toilet without asking, an alien and confusing position for us. He instilled us with music, crafts, nature and a sense of wonderment inside the inhospitable school. I met him many years later; much aged but the same friendly disposition and expressed my thanks which he received with mild amusement.

During those years of deference, going to my grannies for lunch was very welcome. A small figure, with wrinkled face, warm eyes, her hair in a bun, would feed us traditional fare, followed by tea and special pastries bought that very morning. She would always try to buy me a chocolate coconut finger, my favourite. After tea, 3d for spending and 3d for saving, although a Christmas present was usually purchased from the savings. Winter or summer, a very happy and nourishing time was had. We were a special breed, a cut above the rest, and always advised on whom not to talk to. "A bit rough," she would say. This shroud of security was being built, as much a part of your makeup as your genes, laughable in retrospect but part of my roots, so why deny it?

Returning home to a promise of warmth and the security of a warm fire, tea and biscuits, we were never a family of sandwiches. Other kids had jam or butter and sugar, regularly topping up at intervals during our play time. Of course I got my fair share from neighbours but getting provisions from my house wasn't on for the street kids.

A Bump on the Road

Making my way through the narrow terraces and under arches, past little sweet shops with jars of cinnamon lozengers, brandy balls and various concoctions delighting any youngster's eyes, on our way home, we would play and jostle in the wind and rain, or take shelter in shop doorways or under the arch of the town hall. Within the arch a dirty black dirty door that scraped the floor when opened, its dusty windows on either side preventing further light from illuminating the cement staircase. My friend climbed these every day.

Everyone I knew lived in a house with a front door which rarely opened and a back door which rarely shut, unless of course you were a townie and your back door led into a wee yard. My granny had a wee yard, her front door was permanently open, leading to a vestibule door, and everyone announced they were on the way in by saying 'It's only me'. The hall was narrow, with brown embossed paper, worn in the corner by people brushing against it as it was so narrow. The usual holy water font and hall stand that occupied most of the hall, a mirror, hooks for coats and walking sticks, loads of walking sticks. These belonged to Granda. He lost his leg and lung while serving as a batman in the First World War. The man was tall, handsome, neatly dressed with waistcoat and rose at lunchtime, never a man for too much conversation. He expelled his sputum onto a torn piece of newspaper and with a click of his leg, shuffled over to the fire and chucked his trouble in. He had been gassed too, hence his respiratory problems. Frequently I would run to the local chemist for his tablets provisioned in a metal box, the chemist's many cabinets and cupboards now situated at the Ulster Museum.

He dominated his street corner, being over six feet tall, chatting to all and sundry, greeting his grandchildren with a thruppence or sixpence, a charming gentleman. We had been well taught to refuse offers of money and sweets but Granda offered these words: "Never refuse anything that's offered". He was a dapper dresser, waist coat, bowtie, hat and walking stick. My grandparents were respected and loved. They gave so much of themselves. Their influence still binds in many ways.

A Bump on the Road

'Baldy Daddy' was the disrespectful name given to my mother's father. He was a man who did talk, his bald head hidden under his hat. With craggy round features, tiny sunken eyes and soiled overalls, his wired-haired terrier by his side, he would sit on a box covered in potato sacks in the smoke-filled shed used for smoking bacon. His pipe was never too far from his small mouth. Like all pipe smokers I watched him for ages performing with encrusted and stained hands his regimes of cutting and packing the tobacco into his pipe.

Down the cinder path, past a little-hedged garden blocking the view of the house of potatoes and vegetables, we went into the garage. There, my cousin and I sat, as a bottle of stout was removed from the bottom drawer in a battered and bruised barber's chair. With pipe in hand he told us stories of his flying column days, evoking hatred of the British forces in Ireland and the tragic history of our homeland. Tales of gun running, hiding rag-covered revolvers in bridges and trees, we, of course sat mesmerized by these gung-ho stories. True or false they placed a bond between our generations. His death was the first that really hurt. Experiencing emotions not felt before and attempting to explain them to my mother proved impossible at such a young age. She had her own problems; at least that was how it seemed. I think she tried to block things out that hurt as she had no mechanism for working things through. Her gardening helped.

Walking home from school on my own allowed my imagination to fly. I was Robin Hood, hiding from the Sheriff of Nottingham or the Man from Uncle plugging the bad guys. My journey took me over the town's bridge. Here, when the river raged, its arches unseen, trees, and sometimes an odd cow or sheep would get trapped. I'd imagine the town's lower main street had flooded and we were witnessing a battle to save the town, the people and their meagre belongings. I would build rafts and float the town's people to safety, a hero, their hero. Next to the bridge was a saddler, a small warm-faced man sewing in front of a fire in the smallest room. Sawdust covered the floor, and on display, saddles and riding crops littered the Dickensian window. The contented scene often abated with flood and incessant rain. Sandbags placed at his door well to keep the swell out, but many a winter saw the nook flooded. His shop floated to the Ulster Museum too.

My childhood days of playing in the street, kicking the dirt at the side of the kerb or simply using a lolly pop stick to do it for me, watching the coal lorry, black dust and black grainy men, with their bags on the street - these images of idleness gather and fragment. Coal was the main source of heat, the glow of clean pyjamied children after the Saturday bath. The black-faced coal man and the white-skinned children, connected. The coal fire, brass-handled rods and tongs stood sentinel by tiled castellated monuments at the centre of the home.

Fire guards, enclosures protecting the innocent grey-faced inhabitants. Different coals produced difference fires - hot flaming, shooting furnaces or quiet, smouldering smoky curtains. Lighting the fire required craftsman-like skill - sticks, newspapers or a variety of burnable fuels, firelighters, paraffin, twigs. Building the fire was an art in pyramid construction like an Egyptian pharaoh. After lighting the newspapers, scrunched or folded into fire sticks, blowing on the new born kindle to enhance the flaming chances of survival. Pull the damper out a bit, maybe just a little more, an adjustment, a mechanical experiment. The most dangerous moment was yet to come. Carefully positioning a sheet of newspaper over the opening of the fire place, little flames were enticed, producing a crackling dance of shadow and flame behind the thin layer. The trick was to prevent the dance from engulfing the paper. Often it happened. Swoosh, the magic of fire instantly turned paper to a burning sensation, carried hopefully up the chimney.

Children ran out to see the fireworks display from the chimney, when soot exploded into sparks or worse still, the chimney became a flame thrower. The fire brigade's arrival added more fun. We had coal from England, Africa, coke from South America, and slack from god knows where. We had coal-filled sheds, their corners choked with varieties to burn hot, or slow, built close to the back door so that filling up on a wet, windy or snow-driven night was not a major expedition. These sheds were filled all the year round, to ensure our supply of hot water,

A Bump on the Road

cheaper than electricity, or simply stocking up for winter. Local yarns of coal kept in baths and cupboards abounded. We had two coalmen, three bread men and two milkmen, all delivering supplies. This number resulted from my mother being incapable of saying no to any of the relatives.

Those days were generally warm and secure, except when being trained to be toughened up. It was a time when fatherly figures were feared - a young boy grew into manhood with clips, thumps and thrashings - that was the accepted norms. This concept of child rearing had many flaws. Was it simply frustration born out of poor job satisfaction, gambling debts, and a spoilt childish personality? Whatever the reasons for violent temper tantrums, we all felt the back of the hand that fed and clothed us. The genes that replicated, the atmosphere that bred, the family that suffered; it all produced the people we are today. Sorrow followed such eruptions, gently chiding us into good humour, all glad that the monster was now subdued beneath a pleasing personality. Finally tears were hidden and a reserved veil of normalcy ensued. Often the need to put time and space between the explosion and its aftermath resulted in staying in the bedroom for a while, walking through the streets or visiting aunts.

The daily and weekly devotion to religion bore a deep and lasting impact upon the imagination and mind – or soul if you like. One's spiritual life was an extension of the warrior training. My spiritual mentors were lay teachers and men of the cloth – tough no-nonsense blokes, Gaelic men, with soutanes hiding the man within. As preparation for fighting for the faith, one teacher, known for his Christian teaching overseas, routinely strapped us for not going to ten o'clock mass in his parish – not mine. Prayers were said for priests, nuns, brothers, families, deaths, births and for the black babies. We were fighting to save the world from communism, heathens, and of course the Protestants. We marched singing hymns and the Irish anthem, arms swinging, marching to the sweet but dominant voice of the Brother, in a little tin hall named after the Virgin Mary. Left, Left,

A Bump on the Road

Left, Right, Right, Right, all in Irish. Soldiers are we, Sinne Fianna Fáil, into actual memories or memories Irish, of course.

Prepared to do battle, a sporting life, a healthy body, a healthy mind, this was the warrior school of reading, writing and 'rithmetic. It is just I am not one for contact sport unless you include sex. In a corner of a hilly, windswept and damp Gaelic pitch, I avoided contact and potential broken bones as much as possible, trying not to get my new green strip dirty, standing all of three feet two inches.

The Brother approaches; "Ah, you're white as sheet, get stuck in there, run, run," says he in a harsh brogue but not in an unkindly way. This is more warrior-training. He then proceeded to follow me for five minutes. As soon as I could I shouldered a rather fat fellow student (carefully selected for soft body mass), bounced off him, fell to the muddy ground and the Brother was satisfied. Unfortunately I was soaked down one side. The changing rooms were tin huts with the attendant smells of uncouth lumps of youth. It was to be avoided by tiny sensitive boys like me.

Washing facilities were comprehensive - one cold tap over a jaw box. Showers, never mind hot ones, would have been hell. The thought of being naked, exposed to ridicule because your dick was the size of sixpence, no way, thank you very much. I avoided sports for much of schooling, how I don't remember much.

Church and religion, part of school and worship, part from my life. Church and grave yards sat on north-facing hills providing cold-hugging views of town and country. They were a place apart. Despite saying the Rosary in younger days, religion in our family life was muted. Irish Catholic mothers have a reputation for seeing potential priests a mile off. They have innate visions of sons blessing grandchildren. My mother had none of these misplaced dreams. Considering the times and pressures of complete acceptance of the church authority, was she a conscious objector, a free thinker, a forerunner of future generations? Citing claustrophobia and agoraphobia as her problem, an incident from her childhood resulted in her fleeing from the church.

A Bump on the Road

Watching the decaying Latinized version of mass in a decaying church, sitting as close as close to the hot water pipes in the balcony and smelling the sweet wood-varnish of the pews, the ritual of prayer, chanting and singing, at times fuelled my imagination. The chasuble-backed priest with the abundant colour, his stiff-backed, shroud-like appearance reinforced the apartness. The swinging incense held by black and white cassocked altar boys. Sundays - smells of cold damp clothes and bodies mingling with spices of the orient, a paradox of reality, a contrast to dinner of steamy overcooked Sunday chicken and three vegetables. The gilt metal filigree, golden woven braids, silk gothic designs in green or purple, or sometimes the white draped chasuble all belonged to another world, but then was that not their purpose? I H S printed in gold, matching the pair of gates attached to the marble altar rails with curves and arches prohibiting them and us.

Churches are magnificent edifices of architecture, showing the role of the church in the community: dominant, rich, wise. An adornment reflecting the times and people of the past, a continuum of society, built of stone, hard and lasting, internally washed by multi-coloured dust motes. Saints, statues, crosses and fonts fill the air and gaps left in the stonework. Impressive entrances, windows stretching to ceiling with hues of red, blue and gold, genuflection, gothic reminders of the need for salvation, a life beyond tawdry imagination, a saving grace from physical flaws of humanity, a life beyond.

Discovering the local area, playing away from home was a summer occupation, going for long walks by the river's edge, little bits of fishing, watching the fishermen in midstream, galoshes to their waist, moving slowly and steadily, wary of possible holes in the riverbed. The river was generally low at that time year and a favourite pastime was attempting to cross at some point. Jumping onto flattish stones, checking their soundness with sticks gathered and pared into tools of defence should we meet another gang. Venturing from our own turf presented some possibility of gangland feud. Usually it meant running like hell, afraid a Piggy scenario might unfold, being poked by sticks and fingers, or worse, being flung into the river.

A Bump on the Road

Different families, different strokes - my friend's Mum worked during the day, allowing him much greater freedom than I had, so we often played in his house. On entering his stuffy bedroom - curtains still pulled, bed clothes awry, dirty clothes strewn on the floor - such a contrast to my neat bedroom at home with the beds carefully made, windows open to fresh air, nice nylon curtain with folds perfectly placed. Oh for the freedom of a disordered room!

My last year of primary education involved numerous tests and problem solving tasks. Reinforcement came by way of the strap. Each child stood and undertook rapid fire questioning: "Spell reinforcement!" or "Twelve twelve's?" or "If you have twenty apples worth ten pennies each and sell them for twelve pennies each, what profit do you make?" This ritual took place every Friday, our grounding for life in the big school.

The comfortable village life of childhood was somewhat extended to entail the daily trip to the big school. My father knew the necessity of a good education so I was sent to the Christian Brothers in the big city. This was not my first time to experience and inhabit such a place. When I was five years old we had lived in the city of terraces. The streets, some wide and busy, others narrow and dark, were always damp.

During that period we sampled the delights of city life - buses on the doorstep, chip shops on every corner, frequented by courting couples after dark. From the main bedroom we watched boy and girl, arms roving, mouths, or was it heads attached performing an age old ritual we had only seen in American movies. Now they were doing it outside my house. We lived in a three story terrace, in a row of the same, with a corner shop at the end. The other end mounted against the walls of the grammar school. Living here was a contrast to village life, with gardens and neighbours who knew neighbours. A life within, other lives kept out. Here in the city we had steps to the front door and from the back yard. Life lived in tall, narrow twilight, a lack of green space, keeping a house clean and tidy with so many stairs proved uninspiring and tiresome for my mother.

A Bump on the Road

We made friends with neighbouring kids from the mounted terraced houses, substantial double fronted bays railed in by sentinel iron work, others three to four stories high, narrow straight and businesslike, others still sloping towards the river, stepping down into Lilliputian smoke-coloured rooms of fire and kitchen, cramped stairs leading to bed-filled dormitories beneath low ceilings. Fashionable sitting rooms, aspidistra sitting on dolly-covered table, some were so dark that you could barely see. An old gent or lady often sat reading or dozing. Soon we returned to our small town roots, settled in a large-gardened, modern but compact bungalow.

Travelling to the city for secondary school by car allowed time for contemplation, but mostly sleep. I swept past every hedge, house and corner of the fourteen miles. It was a school day journey from September to June passing through the seasons and early adolescence. There wasn't much conversation, just odd comments, like "turn the heater up", or about weekend or school activities. I sat in the back seat dreamily dazed looking out through the mist-covered window at hillocks and the swooping river, glinting occasionally, barely reflecting the cloud-encroached sun.

The atmosphere lightened when we gave someone a lift. Then, talk of current events, football, horses and the weather. Father was a sociable, friendly person to the real world, always affable and knowledgeable. He read two papers, one Irish and one English, a balanced decision reflecting his need for racing information from both sides of the water. His appearance and mood matched his middle-ranking British civil service position, where he was mostly bored. He bought new cars, a practical need for driving daily to work through all weathers.

Every day for years I passed a sloping terrace house down the Folly, its front door ajar to the vestibule, a yellow tiled floor under feet-scraping mats, a brown data rail and ochre coloured walls. In the sitting room sat an old sunken smile, half sleeping. I always waved to him and was furious if he was sleeping, standing there willing him to wake. On occasions he would stand on bent legs, come to the window and tap,

A Bump on the Road

almost expecting to shake hands. Only a few times did my feeble retired parish priest come to the door and wait for me. Two doors down were cottages, seemingly occupied by hoards of people; children ragged, dirty, shouting and older people framed in doorways ready for a natter and a complaint. This row of houses met the school yard wall, used by lunch time footballers. In the middle of this row was a little shop.

The shop had groceries on wall-to-wall shelves mainly occupied with jars of sweets, the usual confection: aniseed balls, brandy balls, butter balls, and the more up market varieties like Quality Street and Ruffles. On the torn lino-covered counter, pennies and small-valued coins passed over adding to its general deterioration. Grubby coins from grubby hands. Placed alongside were bottles of white and red lemonade, sometimes even more exotic: raspberry, shandy, Irn-Bru. Behind this low bench stood the owner, now much taller than me, he had short legs, a regular-sized body, and slightly oversized hands and face. I was small and seeing such a person filled me with a mixture of fear and delight. I wouldn't want to be odd. To the right was a yellowing ceramic bowl where dirty water mixed with dirty glasses. This was my local. Crowded and friendly: I had my daily shot of fire water - my penny drink of lemonade.

The school yard was accessed by a deeply-rutted winding driveway sheltered by a canopy of sycamore and oak. Most of the year, underfoot was a bed of damp decaying leaves. I never saw a car drive up there. The driveway snaked its way up the side of the hill meeting first the primary school, which housed the woodwork room. By means of steps and broad flat cemented slopes one's ascent reaped the reward of a grand view over the Bogside. Terraces of gardens and iron rails laid foundation to blocks of classrooms. Looking down - a vista of neat chain-smoking upon chain-smoking terraced houses. A graveyard could be seen on the hill, little did I know my son would be there before me. The gas yard dominated the foreground, their trucks moving the peak-heaped coal to the silo-like furnaces and banks of offices to the side. This arena below, its grey-moving ceiling contained the most pungent, memory-provoking aroma of burning coals and gas, an ever-present cauldron of sights, sounds and smells. A smell and view easily reproduced in the solid texture of my memory today.

Blocks of classrooms inhabited by thick wooden desks trapped the diminutive unwashed bodies of the young within. Education took place in a twilit world of gruff unthinking men; men and boys locked in the timeless custom of fraudulent scholarship. The enduring basics - reading, writing and arithmetic was the order of the day with monotony-breaking sessions of singing, art and sometimes sport or even swimming. The enforced order of classroom learning laid a lie to the seething masses, the rebellious under body of the student population. Many came from problem homes but little was evident. Besides a few sulphurous bodies and the odd sweep-search for absent students, school days were a tolerable routine. Of course, any spark of spirit was solidly extinguished and proof of stupidity constantly reinforced. Ignorant sons of ignorant sons, a compelling construction of immature minds set in concrete, ready to be forged, needing serious reformation. While this message was driven hard, man to boy, sometimes in a fatherly way, often warrior-like, mentor to his cadet, glints of an optimistic sunny disposition could be gleaned from a few of the suffering souls employed to mould us into Christian and employable citizens. Clerks, tradesmen, perhaps a few university possibilities, horizons were highlighted, dreams even, possibilities of a life beyond childhood and forced education.

Moving to a modern purpose-built school at the dawn of my sexual waking was also a parting from the century-old ways of school. As elder students in a new school where the number of students trebled, we almost achieved sixth-form status, even though examination results proved somewhat disappointing. A hard core of a dozen students, fuelled, I would guess, by their parents' vision that any educational achievement is better than none. These were salad days of school, friendships gained and still remembered, still surviving.

Parties, dances, music, girls and pubs were the sources of our quest. Young men were exercising their need to form friendships and hunt and talk and sing the joys of possibilities! We had little money or style, well, some of my friends were cool and fairly successful with females. We

A Bump on the Road

enjoyed what we had. Destiny was something that was to hold and fixate me in the coming years. Some little voice, some little dream was meandering within my subconscious, my dreamland. It was showing me that horizon, and indicating that was the direction for me. This direction was leaving home and old friends, stepping out to the real world and making the most of it. We left behind our childhood, naively feeling sure of our future steps and the world was for our taking.

Yet time and time again all was swept aside in the reality of death, births and human fragility.